THE ACCOUNT OF MARTIN BRON

THE ACCOUNT OF MARTIN BRON

Freny Olbrich

SIDGWICK & JACKSON
LONDON

First published in Great Britain in July 1987 by
Sidgwick & Jackson Limited

First reprint August 1987

ISBN 0-283-99442-8

Typeset by Hewer Text Composition Services, Edinburgh.
Printed in Great Britain by Adlard & Son Ltd, The Garden City Press, for
Sidgwick & Jackson Limited, 1 Tavistock Chambers,
Bloomsbury Way, London WC1A 2SG.

For Freda

Any man's death diminishes me, because I am involved in Mankind; And therefore never send to know for whom the bell tolls; It tolls for thee.

Devotions XVII
John Donne

GERMANY
Elbe
Maltheurn
Theresienstadt
Hagibor
Prague
Oder
Jauernig
Thomasdorf
CZECHO
Danube
Váh
Inn
AUSTRIA
Sudetenland

Vistula
Bug
POLAND
VAKIA
ROMANIA
NGARY
0
50
100 Miles
0
100
200 Kilometres

Part One Phoenix in Ashes

1

I must be the archetypal wandering Jew. I say this now quite openly because there was a time, a very long time in fact, when I tried to cover up my Jewish ancestry. Now I proclaim it as openly as I did when I was a child. You could say, therefore, that I've reverted to my childhood and dismiss all that follows as make-believe, for weaving fantasies with myself as the central figure was an absolute necessity of my childhood.

My determined attempts to hide my Jewishness were not merely the result of the desire to stay alive. I had no inclination to be a dead hero; in those non-ecological times no one worried about the air pollution caused by six million charred bodies. I hid my Jewishness even before that, merely, I suspect, because I wanted to shed the past and establish my identity in a new place at a new time. And I wanted to be shut of my parents, or, more specifically, of my mother.

Nowadays it is not only acceptable, officially at any rate, to admit to Jewish ancestry in Germany; there is talk that it might be a positive advantage because the German government will pay huge sums of money in compensation to Jews who have lost their homes or businesses. I shall cash in on the deal. Why not? The collective guilt of this nation requires acts of atonement to cleanse itself of the burden of six million vaporized. I shall allow them to do so even though it was not the Germans who robbed me of my livelihood, my home and my freedom. I am a German asking other Germans to set me up again, that's all. All I want is initial capital, not a permanent handout. I have my pride, strange as it may seem – odd, considering I have no scruples about lying, cheating, stealing, whoring, drinking to excess and gambling.

So if you are waiting for a heroic figure you will have to wait till doomsday. I'm no hero, never have been. I'm just a survivor, clinging on, sometimes by my fingernails.

I have only one life to live. If all the pious people I've met really end up in heaven, as they believe, I'm better off in the other place. The irreligious are often better company. Who knows, the devil may be just like one of us: a man who likes to enjoy himself, wants his comforts, loves laughter, and if he gambles with life (as we all do one way or another) is generous with his winnings. I don't believe in a future life any more. I think we make heaven or hell for ourselves here. Or have it made for us. My wife Liese wouldn't agree, but she is a devout, though illogical, Catholic and consigned me to hell long ago. At the moment she is admiring her nylon stockings, a gift which she received rapturously but has never worn because she is afraid she might damage them. I know women who sell themselves for a pair of nylons and strut around exhibiting them, revelling in their novelty and rarity value. But not Liese. She said they were a miracle and put them away in a drawer from which they emerge at intervals to be worshipped. More of her later.

This is the story of something-that-never-happened because it-could-never-happen, which is how truth becomes stranger than fiction. In any war the victors must be blameless; all atrocities are perpetrated by the vanquished alone. Otherwise what are wars fought for?

I, Martin Bron, German citizen, German national, returned to Germany after the war. The American authorities at the border refused to believe my story. 'It-could-never-happen,' they said, and thought I was touched in the head. Over six feet tall and weighing seven and a half stone, I could well have been, but not enough to wipe out the past. I am putting this story down before my memory begins to play tricks on me. In thirty, forty years' time there may be no one left who remembers.

Stalin, Churchill and Truman cemented their friendship after the war at the Potsdam Conference by deciding on the expulsion of all Germans from former German territories in Eastern Europe, Czechoslovakia and Hungary. More than three million of my people died in the resettling process. In the Sudetenland, my homeland, of the three and a half million Germans who had lived there for centuries until kicked out by a man with a moustache, a man with a cigar and a man wearing glasses, just over half a million were killed by Russians and Czechs in the year after the war ended. The rest were expelled according to a policy of deliberate dispersal to different parts of West and East Germany. Beaten, scattered, displaced refugees tell no tales. They have enough to do to survive. I have a wide streak of perversity, of sheer dogged obstinacy in my nature, as Liese never fails to remind me. So I shall do what others have not the time or inclination for: bear witness to what was done.

2

I won't bore you with a detailed account of my childhood. There have been too many attempts at sentimental accounts of childhood deprivation: wearing rags, walking in clogs, living in slumland. I leave these to vote-hungry politicians seeking to ingratiate themselves with the working man. Nowadays every arsehole it would seem, even the most aristocratic one, claims cloth-capped origins – like Hitler. Which only proves that history always repeats itself and no one ever learns from the mistakes of others.

Nor will I try to justify my actions along the lines of the mad Viennese doctor, by what happened to me in childhood. Nothing happened. I did not hate my father or want to sleep with my mother; none of the children I grew up with wanted to do so either.

My parents were German Jews who came from Pressburg, which was part of the Austrian Empire until the end of the First World War, when it became part of Czechoslovakia. So they were first Austrian citizens and then overnight became Czech citizens although they retained their German nationality. I was born in Teschen, which was originally Austrian but became a disputed area between Poland and Czechoslovakia after the First World War, when it was taken over by the Poles although there were mainly Slovaks in this area.

I do not remember Teschen because we did not live there. I was born, as it were, in transit. In fact, we did not live anywhere for any length of time. My parents were constantly on the move. They belonged to a company of travelling actors, most of them German Jews, like my parents, and a small group of Hungarians and

Austrians. My childhood was a very happy one. The constant movement, the freedom, the perpetual novelty combined with my own love of dressing-up, of exhibitionism and applause to make it the best kind of life any boy could wish for.

I was a late and only child, which gave me a very special position with my parents, who indulged me completely, until my mother decided I was being spoilt and felt it was time to discipline me for my own good. I took this as normal, just as I took my wandering life as normal. I had plenty of children to play with; the Hungarian actors had very large families, and we picked up each other's language easily, which was to prove useful later on.

You must not imagine these were highly intellectual actors performing avant-garde plays that no one could understand, the kind that became fashionable in the large cities where the more obscure the play, the greater the credit given it by critics who were afraid to reveal their bafflement. If we had used that kind of material we would have starved. We were never rich, not even well off, but we managed. We were entertainers. Our repertoire was varied but unpretentious: melodramas, love stories, mystery playlets, swashbuckling adventure and extracts from the operettas of Strauss and Lehár, anything that could draw an audience to a village or small town *Gasthaus* and keep them coming for as long as possible. When they stopped coming, we moved on.

We travelled wherever German was the mother tongue: in Bohemia and Moravia, and all over the Sudetenland. 'Over what?' I hear you ask. The most that word arouses, even among Germans, is a vague memory of something associated with Hitler before the war began, a little hiccup in a remote region that was soon forgotten in the numerous cataclysms brought about by the war. The very name 'Sudetenland' has dropped out of our vocabulary and been erased from all maps of the area. But the region still exists. It is a loop along the borders of what is called Czechoslovakia, the area of Czechoslovakia that borders on Austria, the Bavarian Forest in West Germany, the Ore Mountains of East Germany, and what is now the Silesian area of Poland.

If ever there was a never-never land, it is Czechoslovakia. It is an artificial country with an artificial name, created out of what was the Austro-Hungarian Empire at the end of the First World War. The absurdity of trying to create a nation out of an area where 46 per cent of the population were Czechs governing several 'minority' communities – Slovaks, Hungarians, Poles, Ukrainians and, the largest minority of all, the 28 per cent Germans – seems to have escaped the wise men of Versailles. They cooked a stew into which widely disparate elements were thrown and handed it to the Czechs to keep the pot boiling.

I give you this potted history of the Sudetenland so that you can see how legitimate Hitler's claims to it really were (Hitler was an Austrian, reclaiming his own land), as even the British admitted, and because this is where my story really begins, in Waldburg, a long, green valley in the Sudeten Mountains, three kilometres from the border with Germany. We arrived shortly after my twenty-first birthday, at the height of the Depression, in 1931. Tall, blond, blue-eyed, I cut a fine figure in those days even though I had the face of a frog. My face never hindered my affairs with young, and some not-so-young, women. If anything, it made me seem more manly in their eyes; I found I could score more quickly than young men with the profile of a film star. Perhaps my face made the plainest women feel attractive.

I lost my virginity when I was fifteen. Until then I was a total innocent in such matters and believed the older girls in our company when they said they had slipped away 'on business' after the performance when the company mingled with guests at the *Gasthaus*. I was tall for my age and probably looked older than I was. I had a pleasing tenor voice and sang several arias to considerable applause that evening. My mother, who was unusually strict, had only recently allowed me to drink wine, and that evening I drank with others to my success more than I should have done.

The *Gasthaus*-keeper's wife was full of praise for my singing. She led me upstairs to show me photographs of singers at the Vienna Opera House. But, once alone, she behaved in a most alarming way. The more I backed away, the more ardent she became. Something in my face made her ask my age, and I, who even then could lie quite glibly, not wishing to seem a child, said, 'Eighteen.'

At this she began to slip out of her clothes and fumble with my trousers. She was thirty-four years old and built like one of Wagner's Valkyrie. Flushed with wine, astonished at the sight of my first naked woman, I stopped retreating.

After that it was easy. I can see the straightlaced frown when they read this. Shocking! Immoral! Dis-*gust*ing! It depends on how you look at it. If I enjoyed myself with a lot of women, I also gave a lot of pleasure to them. I made them feel, even the plainest among them, in the time they were with me that each was someone special, alluring, beautiful. I gave them a taste of the only kind of immortality I know. And I never took any woman by force. I wooed them and won them, and when they fell like ripe plums into my arms, they chose to do so freely. They all claimed they loved me, but did they really know what that was, any more than I did? I've sung many songs about love, but it still puzzles me. I've desired women, admired them, been fond of them, but I can't really use the word 'love' for what I felt. I'm not sure any longer what it means. Affection, regard, loyalty to my family and friends – these are things I can understand. But love? It is too big a word for me. I do not fit it.

Waldburg would have been just another stopover but it was here that I decided to make the break from my mother. There was nothing about the place itself that made me decide to stay, though if it had been an ugly heap of shacks it might have tipped the balance against my immediate separation. It was a neat, trim place, just large enough to be more than a village, small enough to be less than a town, at the foot of rounded mountains covered in dense pine forests. A river ran through the town, as the inhabitants preferred to call it, which had evolved along its banks with large, two-storeyed houses snug with overhanging roofs. A baroque, onion-domed church stood at the important end of the town.

By the time we reached Waldburg I had realized that my mother was actually a shrew. Ever since I had become too tall to be smacked, she had relied on her tongue to lash me into shape. How she would run on! I timed her once. She could maintain a harangue in full spate for fifty-three minutes. In an attempt to make me a better person than I was, my mother forbade everything I enjoyed doing. She would not allow me to mix with rough children who played all the daring, interesting games while I was made (at least while my mother could keep an eye on me) to play boring, sedate games with the good children who never swore or spat or stole apples from surrounding farms. I was not allowed to get my clothes dirty – a virtual impossibility for an active boy. I learned to invent plausible lies to explain the state my clothes got into regularly. My mother would get angry at even the most harmless lies, so I had to become quite skilled at them. I did not mind these restrictions since I managed to find ways round them. I believed that's what mothers were for. My father rarely interfered with my mother's management of our family; he simply wanted a quiet life.

My release from my parents came by chance. I heard a group of young men talking about leaving for the Czech army. They had just been conscripted for national service. Like all Germans in Czechoslovakia, they had German nationality but Czech citizenship and, like all young men of twenty-one, they had to pay their dues to the state. If I had wanted to avoid national service I could have done so easily. The notice of conscription would have never caught up with me since we were constantly on the move. Which was how other young men in the company managed to evade the authorities. I volunteered for national service and was free of my parents. For two years not even my mother could manage to get me out of the Czech army.

Who knows in what way my life would have developed had I not broken away at that precise moment in that particular place? A man's future is supposed to depend largely on his circumstances and environment. But I chose both, altered them myself. In a sense therefore I shaped my own destiny and can blame no one else for the pattern my life has formed.

3

Much as I hate the Czechs now, I have a healthy respect for their army: thirty-five divisions of well-trained, well-equipped men. No one doing national service ever admits to liking it any more than one admits to liking school, but my time in the Czech army is among my happiest memories. Of course we swore at the sergeant and griped at fatigues, at the long hours, the squarebashing and latrine duty, but it was an active life that suited me. It was also a damn sight more comfortable than the life that civilians had in the Depression. The army provided one of the few places of secure employment. It gave me good food, warm clothing, a modest wage and complete freedom to spend it as I wished.

It also gave me my friends: Max Riedel, Friedrich Weber, Gerhard Neumann and Heinrich Galle. All of them came from Waldburg, except Gerhard, who lived in a neighbouring town. I first met Max over cards. I can see him now, holding a hand at poker, his plump, stubby fingers almost wrapped round the cards, his round, good-natured face trying, without much success, to give nothing away. He had a great, booming laugh, a habit of slapping his thigh with his hand when he was particularly pleased. His father owned a bakery in Waldburg and it took the army some time to trim him down from fat to plump. Heinrich had a flair for repairing machinery. He would spend his spare time poring over bits and pieces brought to him by others, his broad, serious face filled with a brooding intensity mistaken, by those who did not know him, for arrogance. Friedrich played the violin and seemed to live for his music. He made that instrument sing and sigh and weep and dance – truly, he was gifted by the gods. Gerhard was the cleverest of us all and the handsomest:

green eyes and dark hair, with clean-cut, flawlessly proportioned features. He had been in Budapest for several years and could speak Hungarian fluently. He was quiet, unassuming and shy.

The Czech army taught me how to shoot – so well that I became part of the regimental team and won the sharp-shooter's medal for two years. That was a source of great satisfaction to me and all Germans in the regiment. It proved what we all knew: that although the Czechs were the nominal rulers of the Sudetenland, when it came to brains, skill and culture, the Germans won every time. 'Any German is worth a dozen bloody Czechs,' Heinrich always said, and he was right. I say this quite objectively, without rancour, for I did not hate them then. I had no reason to. But now, if you were to show me two roads, one with a Czech standing on it, the other with a deadly snake, I would choose the snake. More of that later.

The army is a great leveller. The Czechs who served alongside us received no special privileges; they ate the same food, got blistered feet, and went on manoeuvres which made them sweat and freeze and drop with exhaustion as we did. The differences between nationalities did not matter until we became civilians again. Although we worked alongside them in the army, we did not spend our leisure time with them. Different nationalities gravitated naturally to different groups and I chose my friends among other Germans.

I was given the chance to stay on in the Czech regular army by my CO. He was a fair man and a good soldier. He offered to send me to the officers' training school to try for a commission. 'You could make the army your career,' he said. 'Finding a job outside will be difficult with so many unemployed.'

I was tempted, very much so; money in my pocket, a permanent job, and one I liked doing. But I refused. For the second time, of my own free will, I altered my destiny. Had I taken up the offer, I would have emerged among the victors in the war, instead of sitting scribbling in this poky little attic coughing my lungs out, and be leading a life of power and influence and considerable comfort. You see what I mean about a streak of perversity in my nature? Why did I throw away such a chance at the height of the Depression, I who had no job to go to, no family firm to accommodate me, nothing? You could well call it an act of lunacy.

My reason was that strange anomaly Czech citizen, German national. My nationality mattered to me. As I explained to the CO, I would not be a very reliable officer in the Czech army; if ever Germany and Czechoslovaka were to be in conflict with each other, my loyalty would be with my people. I would not be able to shoot at Germans or order soldiers under my command to do so either. In addition (and this I did not tell the CO because I did not realize it till much later), I'm too nonconformist to be an officer, not enough of a snob to feel superior to a private because of rank or family connections. I would have been uneasy in that charmed, self-congratulatory circle of privilege and deference to authority because promotion is at stake. I have always had a fundamental irreverence for authority which makes me poor material for a commission. So I missed my chance at greatness and was discharged with the rest of them.

Friedrich wanted to go to the Academy to study music, but times were hard and his parents could not afford the fees. He joined his father's stonemasonry business instead. 'In good times or bad,' he said, 'people need to be buried and want gravestones. I haven't much choice.' His shock of light brown hair made him seem even taller than he was; his ears stood out like a friendly dog's and, at that moment, without his shy smile, he looked as mournful as a bloodhound that has lost its sense of smell.

Max too was assured of a job in his father's bakery. He was delighted his two years in the army were over. Flamboyant and given to clowning, he was always in trouble with the sergeant, always last on parade, last on route marches, last for everything. His weight made it difficult for him to move quickly, so he spent a large part of his time in kitchen fatigues. 'We can't all be good soldiers,' he'd say, his face shining with exertion and good humour. 'I shall become a master baker, marry a raving beauty, who'll wait on me hand and foot and appreciate my talent as a connoisseur of fine wines.'

Gerhard wanted to be an architect, but his parents, like Friedrich's, could not afford the fees. Heinrich's ambition was to work in a garage, but he knew that, like Gerhard and me, he would have to take whatever job was available and let ambition wait for better times.

Civilian life was a shock to us all. The leanness came hard after the abundance enjoyed in the army. Max, with characteristic generosity, persuaded his parents to give me a small room in their house. They would take rent from me, they said, when I found work. I went all over Waldburg and the surrounding area without finding anything.

Eventually it was through Max that I found my first job. Schmidt, the ironmonger, was in the bakery, where he was a daily customer, complaining that his assistant had left for a job in the brewery.

'Probably had enough of the old buzzard,' Max said. 'He's a slavedriver but he pays a reasonable wage, Martin. He's known my parents for a long time. It's a chance.'

One I couldn't afford to miss. I went to his shop immediately and got the job on a month's trial. It certainly was a trial but, with a steady wage coming in (even if the first month was on an apprentice's rate), I'd have worked for the devil himself. I was a shop assistant and general dogsbody. I swept the floor, cleaned the shelves, attended to customers, who were never to be kept waiting, replaced every item sold on the shelves at the end of the day, made a daily inventory of the stock, and ran errands for Herr Schmidt. I had to be in the shop by 7.30 in the morning to open the doors at eight. An hour off for lunch from twelve to one, and lock up at 6.30. Usually I was allowed to leave at 7.30 but once a week I had to stay till nine.

The old buzzard was crafty. He watched me closely and left loose change lying around. Under normal circumstances I would have pocketed it, but I realized he was testing me so I handed it to him with innocent surprise every time. By the end of the month he took me on permanently.

It is difficult to describe the elation I felt on securing a permanent job. It seemed almost incredible, even though I had been working towards it and knew that I had satisfied old Schmidt. I wanted to celebrate immediately but Max was not at home.

I met Heinrich and Gerhard on the High Street. 'Come on, let me stand you a drink,' I said, and would not take a refusal. One drink turned to several and it was a while before I realized they were more subdued than usual and that I was doing most of the talking.

'You were born lucky, Martin,' Heinrich said. 'If someone threw you into the sea, you'd come up with your pockets full of fish.' Something in his tone – regret, desperation, anger – penetrated the aura of wellbeing with which I'd surrounded myself.

'What's the matter, Heinrich?'

He shrugged and said, 'Nothing.'

'He hasn't found a job yet,' Gerhard said. 'It's getting him down.'

Heinrich turned on him fiercely. 'You haven't found one either, have you?'

'No, but I don't take it as hard as you.'

'You want me to sing and dance and clap my hands because I haven't any money even to pay for a bloody beer? Find someone else who can put on an act for you.' He stormed out of the *Gasthaus*.

Gerhard and I stayed on for most of the evening and were joined by Max and Friedrich. We drank to Gerhard's new life. He said he was leaving for Hungary. 'The prospect of a job there couldn't be worse than it is here.'

4

It is time for Liese Groeger to come into this story. When I look at her now I see clearly that her face is incredibly plain, made more so by her faded hair tied in braids round her head, her body a shapeless sack from childbearing, her hands red and rough from housework. But I first saw her through the dazzle of love (for want of a better word) when she was eighteen and slim as a sapling. Her wide-set, wondering blue eyes, her hair the colour of waving corn, loosely tied with a ribbon, took my breath away. I am always more susceptible to women in the spring and summer. Perhaps the blood freezes as the year grows colder. That summer when I met Liese was magical. The sun slanted along the Waldburg valley, highlighting the colours of the landscape with an intensity that made every leaf and blade of grass incandescent. Liese became a part of the beauty that assaulted my senses and was transformed by it.

She worked at the *Gasthaus zum Ochsen*, where I had acted before leaving for the army, cleaning, sweeping, making beds, helping in the kitchen, waiting at table. She had watched all my performances there and adored me from a distance. For her an actor was a glamorous person and she was surprised at how different I looked without costume and make-up. She associated me with the roles I played and made a hero of me. When I tried to tell her I was no such thing, she took it as modesty and loved me all the more for being unassuming. Those who fall in love step outside reason, beyond help.

I was reluctant to visit Liese's parents, as she often urged me to. I knew what that meant and I did not feel ready to settle down as a married man. I valued my freedom too much. Then, it happened.

Liese became pregnant. This had never occurred before with any of the women I had known because I had always taken precautions; or if it had, I had moved on by the time it was discovered. I certainly never had irate fathers pursuing me, so it is more likely that my precautions worked or I was lucky.

Liese was distraught. She could not tell anyone else. Her face was blotched and ugly with tears, her voice became harsh and piercing.

'My father will kill me or throw me out of the house. I'll lose my job at the *Gasthaus*.'

I would have been sorry if any of that had happened, but not sorry enough to sacrifice myself on the altar of matrimony if there had been a way out. Under normal circumstance I would have disappeared overnight to a distant town, left Liese and her as yet imperceptibly thickening body far behind. But times were far from normal. I had had to wait a long time before finding a job; it had been a piece of phenomenal good luck. I knew how demoralizing being unemployed was, saw the ravages it made in demolishing Heinrich, who was crumbling like a building consumed by dry rot. I had become used to money in my pocket, to the freedom, the identity and confidence it conferred on me. It had transformed me from an anonymous being living on the charity of Max and his family into someone who existed in his own right, who did not need to be grateful for daily, commonplace necessities. It had made me independent.

Strange, you may think, that I, who have no scruples, should have been concerned about becoming a parasite. But this was different: it involved one of my friends, and it was a matter of pride which, as you well know, is one of the seven deadly sins, most of which I enjoy in good measure. I needed that pride in order to live with myself; without it a man may as well cut his own throat.

Whenever the Church talks of 'holy' poverty, my gall rises. There is nothing holy about deprivation, hunger and cold. If, as they say, God made man in his own image and this was the best he could do, the devil would have made a better job of it. To talk of holy poverty is obscene and ridiculous, like describing a man whose leg has been amputated as a holy cripple. I had no intention of crippling myself financially; my job was too precious to throw away, as I would have to do if I moved on.

So I did not want to leave Waldburg. I did not want to get married either. I was trapped between two equally uninviting possibilities. And then a man called Hitler tipped the scales in Liese's favour by becoming Chancellor in Germany. He has much to answer for. He did not like Jews, some say because he was part Jewish himself, which perhaps is the strongest reason for disliking them. In Czechoslovakia Jews were mainly found in Slovakia and in the large towns and cities. In Waldburg, apart from myself, there were no Jews at all. Like the rest of the Sudetenland, it was a mainly Catholic region. Here the antagonism between Germans and Czechs overshadowed the inherent prejudice against Jews. The fact that travelling actors were regarded as little better than tinkers had nothing to do with their Jewishness but was a result of their vagabond existence.

The border with Germany was only a stone's throw away and, even in those days, ideas travelled fast. I had shed my parents two years ago. I saw now that I would have to shed my Jewishness too if it was not to prove a serious, perhaps even fatal, handicap. Marrying into a Catholic family was one way of shedding the chrysalis and becoming a butterfly. When that marriage entailed becoming a Catholic myself (for it would not be permitted otherwise) it set the seal on my new identity.

That was how I met Father Johann Klein, parish priest of St Anthony's Catholic Church. Small, slightly built, he had an intelligent, alert face marked with lines of weariness. He was a Jesuit and quite unlike any priest I've met since. He did not lash his congregation verbally as so many German clerics do at sermon time; he spoke quietly, calmly, without histrionics. I went to him for instruction in the Catholic faith. I was surprised that instruction was necessary. I wanted him to pronounce me a Catholic as soon as possible and thought that he would welcome another sheep into the fold. All he had to do was sprinkle me with holy water, mutter his charms and slap on a conversion order claiming me for the Church. He wouldn't have it. I explained why the situation was so urgent. He still refused.

'I must be satisfied that you understand fully what Catholic doctrine means. You must be certain that it is the faith you wish to live by.'

I disliked him immediately. He lived by his faith and expected everyone else to do so. Had he any idea what went on in men's hearts and minds, he who was the nearest thing I ever saw to human goodness and unselfishness? Did he have any effect on the hysterical women who squawked and fluttered around him as they left his church? Simpering and smiling, they deferred to him outwardly in everything he asked. They addressed him respectfully with the dignified title *Herr Pfarrer*, the priest; they bobbed and curtsied and pressed their pious lips to his hand. But all of this made no difference to their daily lives. Devotion and backbiting went hand in hand; strict observance of religious duties and malicious slander made easy bedfellows.

I had stopped believing in God when I stopped being a child. I had never thought much of Jehovah: too much like a stern headmaster to have much appeal for me, a being who used a stick, and enjoyed using it, freely. I thought even less of God the Father. To call him God the Father when my own father was so ineffectual and henpecked was not much of a compliment. The mathematical impossibility of the Trinity simply could not, try as I would, be surmounted. The number 1 never could be 1, 2 and 3; nor could 1, 2 and 3 be reduced to 1 except by elimination. And as for the virgin birth – well, I ask you, can any sane man possibly believe in it? Grimm's fairy tales are more plausible. And even if you admit (in a moment of inspired lunacy) that the virgin birth is possible, why should it happen only once? Why should not the child growing secretly inside Liese have been put there by the Holy Ghost before I ever knew her? Why should not all the illegitimate children in the world be conceived from the Holy Ghost? If one miraculous birth is good, one cannot have too much of a good thing, especially when it is holy. And the mass, the mystery at the heart of the mass, in which ordinary wine was really changed into Christ's blood which the priest drank, and ordinary bread changed into Christ's body which the faithful ate – a gruesome act of cannibalism – how could that be accepted as an act of *worship*?

You see how impossible I found all these concepts which are the bedrock of Catholic doctrine. They go against all reason. Father Klein said that faith had to make a leap into the dark, go beyond reason. He lived by his faith. He wore himself out tending the sick, comforting the dying, bringing God, he thought, to his people in what was to him the renewed miracle of the mass. He had found a kind of peace. It was intangible, an aura he had about him. The words of the mass had become true for him: *Agnus Dei, qui tollis peccata mundi: dona nobis pacem*. It healed and touched and enfolded him, but he could never pass it on to me. He was a man in love with God and, like Liese, beyond help.

So I ceased to argue with him. I lied and accepted everything. I did not mind going to mass on Sundays and holy days of obligation; I found the ritual stirring, the singing of high mass moving. It was an experience I enjoyed, like going to the opera.

5

Liese did not at first tell her parents of the child who was to become my eldest son. Her mother objected to her wanting to marry a Jew. 'Even if he becomes a Catholic people will always think of him as a Jew. Once a Jew, always a Jew. I'm worried for your sake.'

The more she tried to dissuade her, the more Liese insisted on the marriage, until at last the truth was out. Such a scene followed! Such weeping and shouting and breast-beating from her mother, such sullen defiance and so many tears from Liese. Why is it that women always raise such a clamour whenever they are upset? Eve was surely made from Adam's tongue, not from his rib.

Her father was angry and resentful, quite naturally, but realized that marriage would make an honest woman of his daughter and the sooner it took place the better. He even took my part against his wife, praising my conversion as evidence of my love for Liese and my good faith. I liked him. We understood each other. He was a small, plump man with a ruddy complexion, probably the result of free access to beer in the brewery where he worked. His nose was brighter than the rest of his face and almost glowed in the dark.

They had the good sense to keep the knowledge of the child to themselves. So did I. The wedding was arranged for the day after I became a Catholic. I wrote to my parents, addressing the letter to await arrival on the route I thought they would take from the last letter I had received from them. By chance the letter found them. I received a severe reply from my mother in which she said she spoke, as usual, for my father as well. They were far more upset by my conversion than by my marriage. They had always hoped I would marry a good Jewish girl. I knew whom she meant – buxom Annie from the company, whom I could not stand because she smirked at me with covert, possessive looks and ingratiated herself with my mother. I was perpetually getting Annie's virtues pushed at me: Annie the industrious, Annie the marvellous cook, Annie who was a miracle with her needle, Annie who was so helpful, so reliable, such a *good* girl. It's a wonder she didn't marry her herself.

They were disappointed, my mother said, about the marriage, but deeply hurt and outraged by my conversion. In words that echoed Liese's mother, she wrote: 'Once a Jew, always a Jew. You can never be anything else. Never, never, never. This is your birthright. You cannot lose it or sell it or give it away.' So my mother and mother-in-law were closer to each other than either suspected and I was the filling in the sandwich both of them bit into.

My mother knew me well enough to realize that, once I decided on a course of action, I followed it through. Her letter said as much. And to show her grave disapproval of what I was embarking on, she said they would not be able to come to the wedding. It was too far, the journey too arduous, the company's programme too full to allow replacements, and various other reasons which she and I both knew were convenient excuses. I have always found that when someone really wants to do something, he will find a way to do it; if he doesn't want to he will find a hundred and one fictitiously plausible reasons.

However, my mother sent me a lace shawl wrapped in faded tissue paper. It was a family heirloom. Her mother had given it to her for her wedding. It was finely crocheted with delicate patterns of flowers and birds so cunningly woven that they seemed to flutter into life as the shawl was opened out. Strange, to touch that creation and feel my Jewishness stretch back over generations.

I was married in the church with barley-sugar pillars and florid paintings of bosomy females raising their eyes heavenwards to God the Father, whose mane of white hair and beard streamed in the wind, and the bleeding sacred heart of Jesus surrounded by a starburst of gold. I have always hated baroque architecture – so much excess romanticism, such displays of opulent tastelessness, an equatorial forest of marble and stone, the air ringing with the clamour of clashing, aggressive components.

It was a quiet wedding: Liese's family, relatives and friends, and on my side Max, Friedrich, Heinrich and Gerhard, who came over from Budapest specially. Gerhard had done well for himself, married a Hungarian girl and joined her father's building firm. The old buzzard, Herr Schmidt, was there too. I invited him for the wedding so that he would not object to giving me Saturday off – a normal working morning.

After the ceremony we all went to Liese's house, where her mother and aunts had prepared the wedding feast: *Schweinebraten* with *Sauerkraut* and potato salad followed by three different kinds of *Kuchen* – *Streuselkuchen, Apfelkuchen,* and *Käsekuchen* – and the magnificent *Sachertorte* that Max brought from his father's bakery. There was plenty of wine, and Friedrich and two of his friends, one of whom played the accordion and the other the clarinet, provided the music. We cleared the floor and danced and sang old songs.

It was here that I first came across the widow Roth. She was a young woman who had been widowed a week after her marriage, which, as rumour had it, had never been consummated. She maintained she would never marry again. The money her father had left her was enough to let her live in what she considered genteel economy, but was in effect putting on airs and graces to impress those around her with her refinement and apparently delicate nature. She had the status of a married woman without any of its attendant inconveniences. She devoted herself to good works, to the ladies' sewing circle and to the Church Guild. She went to mass every day. She was talking to Father Klein and had her back to me.

'Isn't it amazing, *Herr Pfarrer*, that, of all people, our Liese should marry a Jew?'

'He is a Catholic, Frau Roth.'

'Oh yes, of course. But how extraordinary that he should be so. I mean, whoever's heard of a Catholic Jew?'

'Not so extraordinary when we recall that our Lord himself was a Jew.'

'Surely not, *Herr Pfarrer*!' she said in scandalized tones. She was about to protest when Father Klein became aware of my presence.

'Here is the young man himself,' he said, handing her over to me as he moved to the other end of the room.

She was incredibly ugly, with a face that seemed to have been put together haphazardly out of putty, with a receding chin and a blob for a nose. She jerked her head in sharp, bird-like movements when she spoke, her mouth forming a gash across her face. She gave an embarrassed giggle, uncertain whether I'd overheard her. She bobbed and smiled and made what she thought was intelligent conversation until I managed to drift away on the pretext of looking for Liese. I learned from Liese later on that the only Jews the widow Roth had seen were the bogeymen of her childhood: orthodox Jews with long hair and beards, wearing black, broad-brimmed hats and long coats down to their ankles.

Late in the evening Liese and I went home to our rented flat near the river. It was on the ground floor, two rooms, a kitchen and bathroom – tiny, but our very own. I was king of my castle. On Monday I had to be back at work but Sunday was ours and ours alone.

6

Our eldest son Leo was born seven months later, as robust a 'premature' child as could ever be formed. A year later our daughter Erika arrived, and three years after that our youngest son, Dietrich. Conditions in Waldburg, as everywhere else, worsened. There seemed to be no end to the economic decline that spread like a cancer through the region. Crippling taxes, widespread unemployment and poverty bankrupted many German businesses; they were bought over at knockdown prices by the Czech government and handed over, as a mark of favour, to the Czechs who had fought against Communists in Russia after the First World War, the one people said was going to end all wars. Unless they were self-employed or worked for German employers, there were no jobs for Germans. All state jobs were filled by Czechs; even street cleaners and dustmen were civil servants, and therefore only Czechs could hold these positions.

In German schools, when German teachers retired, they were replaced by Czechs. Children who went to Czech schools were given grants for books and clothing. Those who went to German schools were given nothing. We were Czech citizens in name only – we paid our taxes, we did our national service; for the rest, the business of living, of earning a livelihood, we were very firmly made to know our place, which, in the Czech scheme of things, was at the bottom.

Nothing could be done about this state of affairs. Liese's parents, with others among the older generation in Waldburg, remembered only too clearly the peaceful demonstration against unemployment in the 1920s by unarmed women who were shot in the back for 'causing civil disorder'.

Heinrich became savagely embittered by the years of unemployment. In desperation he joined the Freikorps, an illegal underground guerrilla movement, waiting for the day when they could strike a blow that would bring about union with Germany. He seemed to carry a smouldering coal around his heart; every time I saw him it burned deeper and glowed through his dark eyes, which looked almost black in his pale, broad face.

'The Czechs don't really want us here,' he said, 'but they won't allow us a plebiscite to join the Fatherland. Czechoslovakia owes its existence to the principle of self-determination but it won't allow any other nationality to have the same right. We shall force them to do so.'

Max still worked in his father's bakery, which was heavily in debt. Ours being a mainly agricultural area, the farmers were too poor to buy bread and only did so when they ran out of potatoes.

Friedrich worked in his father's stonemasonry business but that too was burdened with debts. He was married by now and had two children.

'People prefer to spend what money they have on food instead of gravestones,' he said. 'My father's a master mason but has no head for business. He never puts anything in writing. So he gets cheated.'

'Can't you advise him against it?' I asked.

Friedrich ran his long, thin fingers through his shock of hair. 'No one, absolutely no one, can advise my father. He always knows best. I've tried several times. The answer's always the same: "I've built up this business and run it successfully before you were even thought of; I'm not going to change my methods now." I don't know how long he can go on like this.'

Friedrich did not have long to wait. His father lost everything in a disastrous deal with a merchant from Slovakia, a Jew who swindled him. This did not affect our friendship, but his wife Martha stopped speaking to me. Somehow she held me responsible for the ruin that had befallen her family. Liese put aside a small bundle of food for Martha and Friedrich's children: some apples, a loaf of bread, a piece of cheese, a wedge of *Kuchen*. I took it round and Martha opened the door. She was small and stockily built, a hard-working woman who had once been pretty. She bristled with anger.

'Friedrich is not at home,' she said, and was about to shut the door in my face.

'May I leave this with you, then?' I held out the bundle.

She made no move to take it. 'We don't need anything from you,' she said. 'We can manage.'

'Oh, it's not for you. It's for Franz and Maria. Children get hungrier than we do.'

Her mouth tightened, but there was a relenting gleam in her eyes.

'Please, Martha, take it. It's from Liese. For the children.'

She said nothing for a while, then took the bundle and shut the door.

Franz and Maria, who often played with my children, were forbidden to come to our flat until a chance remark from one of them made Friedrich aware of the situation. He brought the children over himself. After that they came over to play as usual and the weekly bundle of food was handed over to Friedrich when he came to visit us.

While the numbers of the unemployed became swollen like a river about to burst its banks, three kilometres away across the border conditions were very different. Under the banner of the National Socialist German Workers' Party (called Nazis by the Socialist Party, whom they in turn called Sozis), a failed painter who had been elected Chancellor of the Third Reich brought into being an economic miracle which transformed a humiliated country into a prosperous and powerful nation. Business was booming there, unemployment was wiped out, public works projects like the great *autobahns* undertaken, and food was plentiful. I, more than most perhaps, have cause to despise him, but even I can see the achievements that made him so popular a leader. Bread and circuses (or mass rallies, as the case may be) are powerful vote-catchers, as the Roman caesars realized long ago. Hitler merely followed in their footsteps. And who knows how different the world might have been had the Vienna Academy of Art accepted his paintings and allowed him his little limited success? Strange to think that my life and the lives of my family and friends, not to speak of the lives of nations, were altered for ever by the decision of a group of academics who thought they knew what constituted art. Did he believe, perhaps, that those who thwarted his early artistic ambitions were Jews?

Max and I were lucky in having a job. It was a shock at the time, but, looking back on it now, I see that my luck could not last for ever. The old buzzard sold his shop because of mounting debts and the new Czech owner did not want my services. I had three weeks before the shop changed hands. Every day I managed to steal some goods and bring them home. By the time I was paid off I had a sizable store: kerosene, candles, matches, hammers and brushes. Liese disapproved of theft. She would rather starve and keep her principles. I felt the goods were better with me than with the new Czech owner. I also knew that principles were no good to a dead man and even less use to his children.

That Christmas was a bleak one, and the months that followed even bleaker. I had married Liese in order to hold on to my job. Ironically, I lost my job and was left with Liese and three children. Trapped, well and truly. Fate is a sardonic jester. Just when I begin to feel pleased about controlling my own destiny, the great axe falls. I have found this time and time again: the gods against hubris, or fate's envious eye on human happiness.

Every day I went from door to door trying to sell the goods I had taken from the shop, all except the kerosene, which was too precious to part with. I sold some candles, matches and a hammer. I tried all the neighbouring farms for work but received the reply given to all who had tried before me: 'Come back in the spring. There might be something then.' All that I achieved through tramping the countryside was to wear out shoe leather.

I went to the woods and chopped bundles of firewood which I sold from door to door, but my customers soon decided to chop the wood themselves rather than pay for it.

I went to the textile mill sixteen kilometres away and bought cheap remnants, off-cuts, seconds and imperfect weaves. I sold several of these but it was a precarious way to make a living. After the initial rounds, business slumped. I had to move farther and farther afield, combing the neighbouring towns and villages. On some days I was lucky; on others I sold nothing at all.

One day I noticed that Leo's shirt had curious buttons; they were dried beans sewn into place. Ericka's blouse had beans on as well. Liese spoke quite sharply when I asked her about them; she was increasingly acid these days.

'Do you know how much buttons cost nowadays? Beans do just as well. But they start sprouting when I wash the shirts. I have to sew a new set after every wash.'

So we lived from day to day, scrimping and scraping and only just managing to get by. Every morning I left on my sales rounds and was surprised that I could still feel the sharp assault of beauty from a landscape that could be so winter-cruel. The trees were wreathed with snow, their branches forming a delicate, intricate network against the sky. Ice floes bobbed and coalesced and shattered in a powdery explosion on the river while icicles hung along its banks forming eerie glacial caverns. The mountains sparkled crisp in the sunlight, a giant backcloth for a hare leaping in the distance, a blackbird alighting on a branch, dislodging a soft shower of snow blossoms, a fox scenting the air tentatively outside its shelter and vanishing in a twitch of its nose.

Friedrich's children had rickets. He hired himself out occasionally, chopping wood for the elderly and infirm, and tried to sell wood carvings that were exquisitely made but which nobody wanted.

Heinrich was still out of work. 'The only one who is able to make a living these days,' he said, 'is filthy Helga. Perhaps we should set ourselves up as pimps.'

Filthy Helga was the town prostitute who had three children fathered by three Czechs. It was difficult to know which was censured more by the worthy citizens of Waldburg: her prostitution or the fact that she consorted with Czechs. The widow Roth was loudest in her condemnation. 'It's a disgrace that she's allowed to live here. She should be driven out of the town.' Fortunately for filthy Helga and her children, although other like-minded citizens talked about her a great deal, they took no action, so she continued to be fruitful and multiply.

Max came round one evening, all the bounce gone from him.

'My father's very ill,' he said. 'He caught a chill last week but insisted on continuing working. He said he'd keep the bakery open even if it killed him. I'm afraid it might do just that.'

His father was in bed with a raging temperature; his mother's time was taken up nursing him.

'Heinrich's out of town,' Max said, 'Friedrich's away in Silesia. We must keep the bakery open, otherwise we'll lose it to the Czechs. I can't cope on my own. Can you help me out? We can't afford to pay you wages, but you can have all the bread you want and lard and dripping to take home with it.'

Which is how I, Martin Bron, actor, soldier, shop assistant, travelling salesman, became a master baker. I started work the next day and found I liked making bread: kneading and pummelling the dough, shaping it and pushing it on long-handled shovels into a huge brick oven, turning out crusty, shiny loaves which filled the air with fragrance. It was work that largely kept me out of the cold and fed me and my family. I continued trying to sell odds and ends in the evening to provide some variety in our diet.

7

In the middle of March that spring of 1938, Waldburg was thrown into a fever of excitement. Austria was free. The long divorce imposed by the powers at Versailles was at last at an end. Overnight, without a shot being fired, Austria became part of Germany. Hitler, who was an Austrian by origin, marched in with his troops.

In Waldburg for the first time in so many years hope crackled like electricity in the air. It was as if the people were being reborn with the thrusting vitality of spring all around them. Even the widow Roth had a smile on her face.

Heinrich was exultant. 'Henlein is taking a delegation of Sudeten Germans to Hitler to present our demands. The Czechs will *have* to agree to our union with Germany now.'

Max and Friedrich agreed with him, but I was not so sure. The Czechs had held on to the Sudetenland for twenty years, refusing repeated demands for a referendum because they knew it would go against them; they were not likely to give their territory away now. Once they agreed to a Sudeten German plebiscite, all the other minorities would demand one as well and the myth of a Czech 'nation' would be exposed for the absurdity it was. And, unlike Austria, they had a formidable, well-equipped army of thirty-five divisions with a large force of reservists.

'What if they don't agree?' I asked.

'Then we'll force them to,' Heinrich said. 'The Freikorps is on full alert.' His broad face shone with conviction. He really did believe that he and his small band of guerrillas could defeat the Czech army. He was the stuff heroes are made of: brave, fanatical, blinded by his vision to the facts, as madmen are.

Henlein returned with a message from Hitler to persuade the Czech government, by every peaceful means, to agree to a referendum. In Austria 99 per cent had voted for union with Germany; we, in the Sudetenland, expected our vote to be 100 per cent.

My fears about the Czech attitude were confirmed. Suddenly frontier posts were closed and armed guards posted there; all civilians were asked to stock up with flour and sugar and surrender their radios to the military. I, with all other reservists, received my call-up papers. The government said they expected German troops to march into the country and were mobilizing against a surprise attack. War with Germany was imminent. Where would the Czech army put the German reservists, I wondered. Right in the front line to be shot at by our own people? Or shot in the back by the Czechs behind us?

Gerhard had come on a visit from Hungary the day before the emergency was declared, bringing luxuries like sausages and coffee for us and chocolates for the children. He was not allowed to return but had to report for army service. All of us were back in the Czech army again.

This was a war that never happened. No invading armies appeared on the horizon. We drilled and manoeuvred and waited in mounting boredom for three weeks. Then, as suddenly as we had been called up, we were disbanded. Gerhard left for Hungary before the Czechs could change their mind. Friedrich, Max, Heinrich and I returned to Waldburg.

The long, green valley shimmered in the summer heat. Wild flowers carpeted the meadows where the grass had grown long and lush. Larks and thrushes scrolled the sky with birdsong. Children gorged themselves on wild strawberries and blueberries, which stained their tongues purple; they ran barefoot everywhere, paddled in the river, tickled for trout or rolled on the grass, wrapping themselves in sunlight. In spite of my increasing difficulties with Liese it was good to be home.

8

As the golden autumn light spilled over the countryside and the landscape flamed in shades of russet, an explosion rocked the town. Sounds of gunfire came from the police station. Two armoured cars of the Czech militia appeared and more firing was heard. The Sudeten German Party had broken off negotiations with the Czech government and given the signal for revolt. The Freikorps went into action trying to capture key installations. Before the day ended the uprising was crushed.

Liese and I were about to go to bed when we heard a scuffling at the front door.

'Don't open it,' Liese said.

'A stray cat,' I said.

But the sound came again, followed this time by faint tapping.

'Who is it?'

'Martin, for God's sake, let me in.'

As I opened the door Heinrich fell into my arms. His clothes were wringing wet, stained with mud and blood. He groaned as I helped him in.

'My stomach. I've got a bullet in it. The signal . . . We got the signal and surrounded the police station. We'd have captured the lot if the Czech army hadn't arrived. It was a bloody massacre.'

'It was a damnfool thing to do.' I was too angry to say any more – angry with him for taking part in such a hopeless task when everyone knew the police station was in radio contact with army headquarters, angry because he could get all of us shot by coming here, angry with myself because I knew I couldn't hand him over to the Czechs.

'I daren't go home,' he gasped. 'They'll be sure to look for me there. I've been hiding near the river. I must have passed out. When I came to, it was quite dark. I'm sorry . . .' He lost consciousness.

'Towels and fresh clothes, Liese,' I said. 'He'll die of pneumonia otherwise.'

Heinrich groaned and muttered in delirium as we changed his clothing. His wound was an ugly mess.

'I must get a doctor to him.'

'You can't, Martin,' Liese said. 'The doctor won't come in the curfew for a man on the run.'

'He will if Father Klein asks him. I'll go to him first.' Much as I disliked the priest, he was useful in an emergency.

Liese's face set in stubborn lines which had become increasingly familiar. 'He can't stay here. It's too dangerous. If the police find out, we'll all be involved.'

'We *are* involved already.'

'He's not worth dying for. He knew the Freikorps was illegal. He must take the consequences. We have the children to think of. Get him out of here, Martin.'

He's got nowhere else to go. We've *got* to help him.'

I left before she could say anything else and, keeping to the shadows, made my way to the presbytery.

'It's dangerous for him to be at your house. We must move him here tonight,' Father Klein said. 'You go home again. I'll bring the doctor to you. It will be better that way.'

When the doctor arrived half an hour later, he said, 'The wound is badly infected. I must get the bullet out. You'll have to help me. Do you have a large table?'

'In the kitchen.'

'Can't we move him to the presbytery?' Father Klein asked.

'Out of the question. He needs immediate attention.'

We moved him to the kitchen and Heinrich, who was so good at repairs, became a piece of machinery which had broken down and had to be dismantled before being restored to working order again. It was a long, slow process. As the doctor was putting in the final sutures, Heinrich stopped breathing.

The doctor swore and tried to revive him, but Heinrich had gone, slipped away while we were busy putting him together again.

'I'm sorry,' the doctor said. Shock after surgery. It's always a risk.'

'You'll make out a certificate?' Father Klein asked.

'Yes. Cardiac arrest.' He exchanged a glance with Father Klein which implied that that would raise no questions.

Heinrich looked strangely relaxed in death. His broad, pale face was free of its habitual intensity. The tension had gone out of him and he seemed years younger, like a boy of seventeen. It was a pointless death. What had he been after in the Freikorps? Heroism? What was so heroic about a gutted carcase lying on a kitchen table? He had thrown away his life in a meaningless act of bravado. Heinrich had thought it a great honour to be invited to join the Freikorps. The Freikorps – the death-and-glory boys. Boys playing with a few guns, charged with the excitement of a secret society. They believed they could take on the disciplined might of the Czech army. Anyone could have told them they didn't have the chance of a snowball in hell. They were so inept. Only a month ago one of their own men had shot another during manoeuvres in the woods. 'A man can't even go for a quiet pee in the woods without getting his arse blasted off,' Max had said, and Heinrich had taken a long time to live that down.

'I'll inform his parents,' Father Klein said. 'We must bury him tomorrow.'

Just seventeen days after Heinrich's death the Sudetenland at last became free. Not a shot was fired, not a man lost. It was all done smoothly through diplomatic channels at Munich. Britain, France and Italy made our union with Germany possible in spite of everything the Czechs did to prevent it.

In Waldburg celebrations went on round the clock. German flags waved from every window. German troops marched in and were welcomed like brothers. Czech civil servants moved out into Czechoslovakia; Czech shopkeepers sold up and left.

Max produced wine from his cellar and we drank far into the night.

'To Germany,' Max said.

'To German citizens, German nationals,' Friedrich said.

'To 1938,' I said, 'and all the years to come.'

I should have known better. The envious gods were listening.

Part Two Phoenix Reborn

9

The new regime brought many changes to Waldburg. It was a time of great happiness for all Germans. We were free. We were masters of our own destiny. How foolish that seems with the wisdom of hindsight, but that was how we felt at the time – like prisoners from a dungeon, suddenly released into sunlight. The large unemployed labour force was mobilised and provided with work: some on the land, some in building projects, the largest of which was a brick factory on the edge of town, others on new roads connecting the factory to the main highway. German schools now had German teachers; our civil servants were now our own people. How can I describe to you what this meant to us, this birth into freedom, this coming at long last into our inheritance? Only the dispossesed will understand, only the exile and refugee will appreciate fully what it means. We had been living like cripples and were now allowed to walk.

In that fleeting year we enjoyed a prosperity unknown in the valley. The economy picked up rapidly. *Kuchen* of all kinds appeared in the baker's shop, while the supply of fresh bread was sold out by mid-morning. 'We have no bread left,' I said, 'but we can give you cake.' And now the people could afford to buy bread *and* cake. Marie-Antoinette said much the same thing, only she lost her head over it. The bakery was doing so well that Max's father had to employ extra men and was able to buy a car. The farmers, who had lived on potatoes, were now among his best customers. My job at the bakery became permanent and, what was more important, had a good salary attached to it.

I no longer needed to be a travelling salesman but I was able to supplement my income from the bakery from another source.

Under the Czechs church taxes had been collected by the state and then passed on to the Church. Now they were made the sole responsibility of the Church. Father Klein offered me the job of tax collector for the Catholic Church in the Waldburg diocese. Being a tax collector is the next best thing to being the public hangman, but at the time I did not think about anything else except the extra money involved. Most of the parishoners paid their dues at the presbytery. My job was to go to the homes of those who had forgotten or who preferred to pay at home. It was easy work, involving only one afternoon a week, and meant that I came to know a large number of Catholics, and they in turn knew me as a church official. It had distinct advantages in establishing my Catholic identity, so I took it.

In spite of our economic prosperity my difficulties with Liese continued. Why is it that I am always made uncomfortable by excessive goodness in a human being? Father Klein was a good man whom I admired but also disliked intensely. Liese is a good woman but I have never felt comfortable with her. She did everything anyone would expect of a good German *Hausfrau*: she cleaned and scoured and sewed and cooked – and had not another thought in her head. It became impossible to talk to her about anything except the house and the children. She has a habit of making extremely dogmatic statements on no evidence at all. She regards a difference of opinion, a different point of view, as an attack on her personally. She resents it bitterly and, forgetting the point under discussion, will retaliate with a personal attack. All women should be taught how to reason logically before they are allowed to get married. A man simply has no chance otherwise.

During the years of the Depression I stole, I lied, I cheated, and Liese condemned me for all of these. 'How can you be a good Catholic and do such things?' she said, her lips tightening in a thin, disapproving line.

'Does it make me a better Catholic if I allow you and the children to starve?' I replied. 'I'll sup with the devil himself in order to survive.'

But she could not see this and put me in the doghouse. She actually said that she would pray for me! This really annoyed me. It implied a superior moral stance from an inferior and illogical mind. I shouted at her in my anger; sometimes I was so exasperated I nearly hit her.

Liese became mean with money. Perhaps it started with the need to watch every *Heller* she spent when times were hard, but she watched every *Pfennig* even when there was no longer any need to do so, which makes me think that she is mean by nature. She condemned my gambling, which was unreasonable since *I* earned the money I gambled with and it was usually only a small part of my wages. I enjoy a little flutter. Risk nothing, gain nothing. Liese despised it because she said it was immoral to get something without deserving it. Christ in heaven, if we all got only what we deserved most of us would have a thin time of it. Why should we not give fate or fortune or the gods or whatever powers govern our lives the chance to be generous? But Liese could not see this, and it was the cause of frequent disputes between us. She resented it if I had a drink or two (especially if it was three or four), and was unduly strict with the children. She said she loved them and I believed her, but she nagged them all the time, and when she wasn't haranguing them she was berating me.

'You disapprove of everything,' I shouted at her. 'No one can do anything right, no one, except the priest. Perhaps you should have married *him*.'

She was scandalized. She was so enraged that she went to the other extreme and did not speak to me for a whole week – which had its compensations. Meals were served in heavy, injured silence. She clattered the pots and pans loudly when she washed up. Afterwards she sat opposite me with a face like an open grave. All my attempts to approach her were repelled.

'I'm sorry,' I said.

'You're *always* sorry,' she retorted. 'It's not enough.'

She would not allow anyone to say a word against the Church or its priest.

'I was born a Catholic and I'll die a Catholic,' she said in the early days of our marriage. And I was appalled by this, by her total certainty that embraced a lifetime and wiped out change. How *could* she have a mind so certain, so closed? I envied her her certainty as well. It made the tangle of living so simple. I have never been able to claim such assurance. But then, I'm a total pragmatist, leapfrogging from creed to creed.

'You're the last person to talk against the Church, after all it's done for you,' she said.

And she was right. But the fact that it had helped me shed my past could not make me close my eyes, and my mind, to its absurdities and inconsistencies. It was madness to produce any more children when we had so little to eat in those days before 1938. Even Liese saw this, and yet the Church and Liese would have nothing to do with preventive methods, which it called sinful. She would not have anything to do with me if I wore *Blausiegel* – what the English call 'French letters' and the French call 'English letters', but then those two countries have always been the best of enemies. Everyone knows that *Blausiegel* are not 100 per cent reliable – after all, the one that produced Leo must have had a special papal blessing – but to do without them is to invite a whole army of children into the world without the means to feed and clothe them. That to me is really sinful, downright criminal.

Liese would have nothing to do with me without *Blausiegel* either. The Church advocated total abstinence, and this, said Liese, is what we must practise. Women are evidently different in their sexual drives. Liese would get into bed with me, yet insist on total abstinence! I found this impossible. I don't know how priests manage, whether they play with themselves to release the fierce drive in a normal man or have such enormous willpower that they deliberately suppress, and eventually kill, the fires within them. But I'm not a priest, or a plaster saint. I'm flesh and blood, and it's more than my flesh and blood can stand to be denied its natural outlet.

So I looked elsewhere in the town and found my pleasure. Liese knew this and harangued me for it. I found this dog-in-the-manger attitude infuriating. She did not want more children; she did not want me to wear *Blausiegel*; she did not want me without it either; and she did not want me to go to other women. She was all negatives, all prohibitions, all disapproval. I was forced to admit the awful truth that, in marrying Liese, I had in fact married my mother: the same censorious nature, the same obsession with children, cooking and religion – *Kinder, Küche, Kirche* – to the detriment of everything else. I had well and truly been caught in a web of my own making.

10

Waldburg became a thriving country town, but incredible prosperity brought with it other changes. Crude propaganda posters denouncing 'the evil Jew who sucks the life blood of the nation' had not yet arrived in Waldburg, but we heard of Crystal Night, the Night of Broken Glass, when synagogues were burned, Jewish property destroyed and thousands of Jews arrested – the number killed was unknown. It was the beginning, as we did not discover till the war was over, of Hitler's 'final solution to the Jewish problem'.

In Waldburg, as everywhere else in Germany, the Catholic scouts and cubs were disbanded. Instead we had the Hitler Youth for boys over fourteen and its junior branch, the German Youth, for boys over ten. Girls were not left out: those over fourteen joined the League of German Girls, those over ten its junior counterpart. Enrolment in all these was compulsory, like joining the Young Pioneers in Russia.

My eldest son Leo, who was only five, could not wait to join the German Youth. He had seen them marching in their smart uniform: black shorts with a leather belt, brown shirt, black neckerchief, white socks and, best of all, the thing Leo coveted more than anything else in the world, a sheathknife with a handle carved with the emblem of a swastika within a diamond. How powerful the glamour of a uniform is to a small boy. Leo pestered me for weeks on end for a sheathknife; he had a good measure of his mother's stubbornness. I bought him black shorts but, for the rest, he knew he would have to wait for centuries to pass before he was ten years old.

Leo heard all about the German Youth from friends who had older brothers at school. They met every Saturday afternoon and their first activity was a test on Hitler's life and deeds, which they had learned by heart and rattled off to their instructor, one of the older boys from the grammar school. This was pretty boring, his informant admitted, really tedious, as was the marching and squarebashing that followed. But the rest of the afternoon was spent in ball games and races. Sometimes they had earth fights arranged between two teams who threw clods of earth at each other. Leo thought it was a marvellous idea. He got together some friends and arranged an earth fight of his own in a neighbouring field. The farmer did not take too kindly to this: he came rushing out, chased the boys away and threatened to call the police.

On Sunday mornings, when attendance was voluntary, they had film shows in the sports stadium or 'army manoeuvres' in the woods, a far more exciting way for children to spend Sunday mornings than at mass. It was as well for Leo he was too young to join, for Liese would never permit any of the children to miss mass. So my eldest son, with his laughing, mischievous eyes and close-cropped, blond hair had to make do with dreams filled with uniforms and knives of all shapes, with beautifully carved handles and blades so sharp they could cut the fine golden hairs on his arms with the whisper of a stroke. Waiting to grow up is, of all things, the most difficult for children.

In the spring of 1939, 20 April was a public holiday. It was Hitler's birthday. Flags were out all over Waldburg. All secondary-school children assembled in the school hall with the school band, and marched four abreast along the main street to the sports stadium. Here they were welcomed with a speech by one of the leading lights of the National Socialist Party who paid tribute to the Führer and urged everyone to live up to his ideals: to grow up strong and pure, to work for the common good with dedication and a total disregard of self – the usual bumf politicians hand out when they speechify.

The rest of the morning was given over to songs and gymnastic displays. In the afternoon there was a party for mothers and children under ten, with cakes, lemonade and balloons. It was the first time my children ever attended a party and, after the war started, it was the last.

11

One Sunday afternoon, after yet another futile argument with Liese over my gambling losses, I stormed out of the house and walked into the woods to clear my head of anger and exasperation. I wanted to be alone, not to hear the sound of a single human voice, least of all a shrill female voice. The silence of the woods is a great healer: it enfolds and balms the bruised spirit. I went deeper and higher up the mountainside, the scent of pine needles, the clean air of the mountains, all around me.

I was just beginning to shake off my anger when I heard shouts and screams from a nearby clearing. I moved closer and saw a ring of men beating up someone inthe centre who was screaming, 'Help me, help me, someone! Help me!' in Czech. Had I not already been very angry I would not have intervened – there were four men around him and, strong as I was in those days, four to one is not very good odds. But my anger got the better of me and I ran forward shouting, 'Leave him alone.'

The group clearly did not expect to be discovered and stopped in surprise. I recognized them: three of them were Heinrich's friends; the fourth I knew by reputation as the local bullyboy, Joseph Katzer, bullet head, beady eyes, thickset like a bull. The man on the ground was short and dumpy, his eyes those of a trapped animal. His mouth was bleeding, his face badly bruised, the flesh around one eye blue and purple. It was Wazlawik, a former Czech customs official.

Heinrich's friends looked embarrassed.

Katzer was not. 'Oh, it's you, Bron,' he said coolly. 'We're teaching this Czech swine a lesson. Want to join in?'

'What's he done?'

'Thrown his weight about for years. Confiscated brandy, tobacco and other goods, which he no doubt kept himself and made a profit on.'

'That was his job.'

The Czech whimpered, wiping his mouth on his sleeve.

'If you're not interested, keep out of it,' Katzer said. 'This is Freikorps business. We've been kicked about by Czech bastards long enough. It's our turn now.'

'Four to one?'

'Are you a Czech arse-licker?' Katzer snarled.

'No, nor a coward either. I despise the Czechs as a nation, but I see no reason to take it out on one individual.'

'I'll do what I like, you filthy Jew.'

At that I went straight for him, the full weight of my body behind my fist. He crashed to the ground but got up quickly and grappled me about the waist. I brought both hands together around his neck and squeezed till he was forced to let go, then brought my knee up into his face and disabled him with a kick in the groin.

Heinrich's friends drifted away. The Czech stayed where he was, whimpering. He looked at me but said nothing.

'Go!' I shouted at him. 'Get out of here, as far away as you can. Now!'

He got up, holding his left arm awkwardly against his side, and half limped, half hopped, as he scuttled away.

Several weeks later I was on my way home after collecting taxes from the owner of a large, square house on the edge of the town. I had been there four times before and each time the owner had produced a fresh excuse about the difficulty of paying his dues. This time, however, he'd had the money ready for me and I was feeling pleased with myself.

Before I reached the main road, four men barred my path. It was Katzer and his drinking companions, not the three I'd seen him with the last time.

'Gathering taxes?' Katzer said, his face ugly with pleasure. 'The money goes in your own pocket, doesn't it?'

'You can check that from the church accounts,' I said.

'I don't need to. I know. And I'll show you what we think of bloody Czech-lovers.'

I grabbed the smallest one of the bunch and sent him sprawling. The two other uglies moved round my back on either side, while Katzer moved in from the front.

'Hold him,' he said. 'Call for the Czech swine you protected to save you now.'

Long before they had finished with me, I passed out.

News of the attack spread quickly in Waldburg. As a result I acquired the reputation of being a pillar of the Catholic Church. Katzer and his friends earned almost universal condemnation. In several small, insinuating ways it was made clear to them that they were an element the town disapproved of. They had a visit from the local police, who made it plain that in any future incident they would be under immediate arrest, with or without witnesses. They now sat by themselves in church. Max's bakery always ran out of bread whenever they called.

Only the widow Roth went against the tide of public opinion, as Liese discovered from one of her friends. The widow Roth invited her friends in regularly for coffee and *Kuchen.* She took inordinate pleasure in being the first to air a scandal or present a piece of gossip. She always liked to be in the know, her blob of a face stuck forward like a turkey cock's, her eyes round with astonishment or excitement or condemnation or triumph, depending on the nature of the scandal to be divulged. There they sat, week after week, the large-bosomed ladies in their frilly blouses, stuffing *Apfelstrudel* into their mouths and clucking their tongues, this time, over me: 'Poor man! Poor man!'

'I think,' said the widow, dabbing her lips with quick pecks of a table napkin, 'any normal man would have hit back and not allowed them to get away with it. The honour of the Church was at stake. But then,' she sighed, 'he's not *really* one of us, is he? He never has been. It's only what you'd expect of a Jew.'

One of the large ladies did mention that I was overpowered by numbers, but the widow said, 'We only have *his* word on that.'

The rest of them did not protest. They could not see how the honour of the Church came into it but did not want to be thought stupid or ungrateful – after all, they were guests in the widow's house – so they did not argue or contradict her.

12

Summer . . . summer . . . That sumer before the war – is it a trick of memory that makes it stand out as glorious merely because it is softened by distance, an imaginary fragment when time stood still, an enchanted interlude heightened by the succession of horrors that followed? I remember it as the best in years, when earth and sky and mountains hummed with sunlight, wild flowers blazoned the meadows and trout glided silently in the clear, flashing river. I remember lying in the cool woods on beds of pine needles, a lovely girl in my arms, while the sky flamed to gold and faded to soft pastel in the long suspended twilight.

News of war broke like a thunderbolt. It seemed impossible to believe. In this peaceful valley, so remote from the great cities where men carved out the destinies of nations, which concerned itself with its own affairs, which asked only to be left alone to work for and enjoy its newfound prosperity, the notion of war seemed preposterous. What made it all the more baffling was that the English had declared war on Germany. Great Britain, which had always been admired and respected as a country which understood Germany and had been responsible, in a large measure, for setting the Sudetenland free! How could she do such a thing? Why did she do it? It was a form of betrayal, as if a staunch and trusted friend had gone mad and stabbed one in the back.

To this day I don't understand it. Why? Because of Poland and German troops marching in to reclaim the corridor? It doesn't make sense. I could have understood if they had declared war over Austria earlier on, or even over the Sudetenland, which the

Czechs showed no inclination to part with. But for Poland! What doth it profit a man if he lose his own soul and gain Poland? And not even the *whole* of Poland, though heaven knows even that wouldn't be worth a war. But for a strip of Poland, a narrow piece of land that had belonged to Germany originally, and where the population was almost entirely German, a corridor that cut East Prussia off as an island from the rest of Germany. The Poles think they did well out of this war. They gained a large amount of German territory to compensate for a larger amount of their own land in the East which the Russians took from them – and lost their freedom to the Russians.

Liese's parents took the news of war badly. They remembered only too well the previous war and the desperate hardships it brought in its wake. Politicians plan campaigns and strategies and alliances as if they are playing with pawns on a chessboard. 'The people' – all in the name of 'the people,' who suddenly acquire importance only in times of elections or war. Liese's parents did not believe they could survive such a cycle again. The news of war wiped out their future.

'It will happen again, it will happen again,' Liese's mother moaned, rocking backwards and forwards. 'We shall lose everything, and this time we shan't live through it.'

Liese's father became silent and withdrawn. He took to drink, drank himself into a stupor to blot out what could not be faced.

Gerhard had been caught once again on the wrong side of the frontier. The borders were closed and he was not allowed back in Hungary. All he could do was wait for his call-up papers.

Friedrich and Max were both reluctant to go to war, Max because he loved his comforts too much and Friedrich because he had at last found a steady job in the timber mill. Of my small circle of friends, Max was the only one still unmarried, although he was the one who would have best been able to support a wife.

'Are you determined to remain a bachelor, then?' Gerhard asked.

'Of course not. I just haven't found a woman who deserves me yet.' He became unusually serious. 'The war's not the best time for permanent relationships, is it? When it's over, why then . . .' He shrugged off his momentary gravity. 'Then I shall find a beautiful woman with a large fortune and we shall set up a *Gasthaus*. *She* will run it, of course, and feed me *Jaeger Schnitzel* and potato salad every day while I . . . supervise things generally and share our superb wines with our customers.'

'Your fantasies grow every time you mention the subject of marriage,' Friedrich said. 'The last time your wife was just going to be beautiful and a marvellous cook. Now she's an heiress. By the time the war's over she'll have become at least a princess or even a queen.'

I was the only one who welcomed the war. It came at exactly the right time for me. It provided my escape from Liese. If my call-up papers had not come as soon as they did, I would have volunteered.

On the day before I left Liese insisted that we all go on the annual pilgrimage to the shrine of the Virgin at Mariahilf. It was far up in the mountains and meant a whole day's excursion. Pilgrimages and saints meant nothing to me. Might as well go on a pilgrimage to a rock or a tree stuck somewhere on a mountain. However, I agreed and we joined the crowds all moving in the same direction. Up and up we went through the woods, passing old women hobbling along on sticks, a sprinkling of old men, and several women who carried penitential sacks full of stones on their backs. Nothing would satisfy Liese but she too should fill her sack with stones and trudge upwards weighed down by them.

'Do you really think carrying stones up the mountainside will wipe out your sins?' I asked. 'Do you feel these are enough or shall I fetch some really heavy stones as a kind of insurance, an extra premium for future sins?'

'You would do well to carry some for yourself,' she said severely.

At the top, outside the chapel of Mariahilf, a fair was in progress. Stalls were doing a brisk business with rosaries, medallions and religious trinkets for the devout. For the children there were toy trumpets, kaleidoscopes and a myriad glittering gaudy objects like the Virgin Mary in artificial snow.

We stayed there all day. The children played, I lay under a tree, secluded from the fair, with my companion from the woods, and Liese did a lot of praying in the chapel. The next day I went off to the war.

13

I will take you with me back into the German army and let you see something of how we lived and fought. *Why* we did so has as many different reasons as there are men. I can only explain my own.

Killing in war is a job – not quite like any other, but near enough as makes no odds. I was not fighting for a cause and certainly not for the Führer, who had already killed so many of my people for some grand design of cleansing the world and producing the master race – which is fine unless *you* happen to be classified as the vermin to be exterminated. What was I fighting for? Nothing so grand as freedom or honour or patriotism. None of these big words fitted me; I leave such terms to politicians. I was fighting, quite simply, for myself – for my survival and that of my family. It was either the enemy or me: a simple equation in which one side had to be eliminated, and I was going to make damned sure it was not me.

So I became an efficient killing machine. There was nothing personal in it. I couldn't even summon up hate for the enemy, whatever the propaganda spouted. In the German army we left hate to the SS, Hitler's personal political army, which had no connection with regular soldiers except to spy on them and report to their master.

'How could you do it?' I hear you ask. 'How could you kill another human being? You especially, who do not believe in an after-life?' The notion of the sanctity of human life is a luxury cultivated in peacetime. Like anything else, killing is easy after the first time. But the first time, I must admit, was difficult even for me.

The first person I ever killed was during the advance on

Boulogne. I came upon him suddenly and we stood looking at each other (perhaps he too had not killed before), surprised to see the enemy look so human. It seemed a long time but it must have been only a couple of seconds. As soon as he moved his hand I shot him straight through the heart. He had a round, freckled face and fine, dark hair. He couldn't have been more than eighteen. I stood there paralysed, appalled at killing a boy, a mere child.

Fortunately there is not much time to stand and philosophize on a battlefield. You kill quickly, as many as you can. You do not lose pity; you learn to live without it, for pity is the most dangerous of all emotions in war – it can cost you your life. You do not lose fear, whatever the braggarts may say; you learn to live with it. A man who says he knows no fear is either a liar or a lunatic. So, very quickly, I could see half a skull blown off, men with their guts spilling out of holes the size of craters, boys separated from their legs like circus freaks, and pass them by to get on with my job. I dreamed a great deal in those first weeks of my fiery initiation – nightmares of choking, burning, running with no escape – but after a while the dreams stopped. Exhaustion is a great cure for dreaming.

My war began in Boulogne, which we took after fierce fighting from the French. We had already crippled the Belgian army and expected to meet the combined forces of France and England, but we found no English there. For a day and a half the French fought us like lions, only to discover that, while they were fighting, the English forces – two battalions of Foot Guards – had left by sea without informing them of their departure. At Calais the English Light Infantry fought ferociously before surrendering. But at Dunkirk the betrayal of Boulogne was repeated against the French.

Dunkirk was the most curious event in the whole war for me and has remained an enigma. I shall never understand the English. Every year they celebrate this most ignominious defeat as a great victory. The French and Belgians, whose soldiers died while the British ran from Dunkirk, cannot understand it either.

We had the French and British boxed in at Dunkirk. We were about to give the *coup de grâce* and capture a large part of the

French army and the whole of the British army. By then our armies had already conquered the whole of Europe, except France, in the *Blitzkrieg*, the lightning war. The whole British army was ours for the taking. The war would have ended there and then. And yet, for some reason that has never been explained, we were ordered by the High Command to halt our advance. Hitler and the High Command, the old generals sitting at their polished desks, knew better than our own commanders in the field. This was the first time I experienced a state of affairs that was to be repeated over and over again in the German army – Hitler and his desktop generals in Berlin always knew better than the specialists in the field. Ordinary soldiers follow orders regardless of where those orders come from.

So we sat and waited and watched, as thousands of British soldiers slipped away in little boats across the sea and the French stiffened their defences on the western sector. Bad weather kept off the Luftwaffe; when they eventually arrived most of their quarry had escaped. Perhaps Goering was too busy powdering and perfuming himself to send out an effective attack. Perhaps Hitler felt magnanimous towards the British whom he always admired. Who knows? Whatever the reason, it cost us the war.

By the time we were allowed to advance, most of the British army had escaped. After ferocious fighting, the French surrendered – 40,000 of them.

'Where are your English allies?' I asked one of them who could speak German.

'They're all in England,' he said bitterly, and spat on the ground.

'Why did you not go as well?'

'We did not know they had betrayed us,' he said. 'They ran, and left us to do the fighting.'

More French soldiers surrendered on the beach, where they had been left after the last boats had gone. They had heard rumours that the British were leaving and tried to leave as well, but in the first six days of evacuation they were not allowed on the boats, which were reserved for the British. Several of them saw their comrades thrown off the boats they had managed to climb aboard. We learned that about 100,000 Frenchman had got away in the last days of evacuation. Perhaps Dunkirk saw the birth of the Frenchman's view of England: 'perfidious Albion'. It is not surprising that the French will never trust the English again.

Our radios picked up the BBC's report of Churchill's speech after Dunkirk: 'We shall fight on the beaches, we shall fight on the landing grounds, we shall fight in the fields and in the streets . . . Our empire beyond the seas . . . will carry on the struggle, until, in God's good time, the new world, with all its power and might, steps forth to the rescue and the liberation of the old.'

We laughed ourselves sick over this. It only proved what I've always maintained, that those who frequently call on God are the biggest charlatans in the world. Here was England's half American, cigar-smoking Prime Minister pulling the wool over his people's eyes. We did not need Goebbels to tell us of the lies British propaganda produced; we heard them for ourselves. Churchill was proclaiming a defeat as a victory, threatening us with his mighty empire, and making flagrant overtures to America to help him out of the mess he had got himself into.

Allowing for differences of nationality and temperament, I see now that there was little to choose between Hitler and Churchill in monumental folly. Hitler failed in his attempt to gain an imagined empire and lost a large part of his own country as a result of the war. Churchill lost the vast empire he already possessed, which had been built up painstakingly over three hundred years. Both Hitler and Churchill were superb orators, consummate con men capable of rousing, and duping, their people in different ways. The only one who did not need to persuade his people with oratory or histrionics was Joseph Stalin. In terms of actual territory and power, he alone was the victor in the war. And it was Hitler who was responsible for bringing together Churchill and Stalin, that great champion of democracy and freedom. After all, they were fighting for the same thing, weren't they, the 'liberation' of the world?

14

The next phase of my war was spent in the Afrika Korps commanded by a general who has now become legendary, whom Hitler ordered to commit suicide and then gave a state funeral with full military honours. General Erwin Rommel – no desktop general this one. He led his men from the front always, at the spearhead. He was a man in love with war. He had already fought in the First World War and as a young lieutenant won the highest honour of all, the Blaue Max. When we came to serve under his command he was already fifty. We called him *der Alte*, the Old Man; even I, who was thirty-one, did so.

We were told we were being sent to North Africa to help the Italians out of the difficulties they had got into with the British. We expected to mop up quickly and move elsewhere. I was a sergeant by then, in charge of a platoon of youngsters, eighteen years old most of them. The lieutenant in charge of our company was Peter Richter, who was twenty-eight, tall, with unruly dark hair, features as fine as a girl's; he always carried a copy of Homer's *Iliad* in the original Greek. We called him the Professor because of his serious, scholarly face and because he could read fluently, and swear in, Greek and Latin.

My platoon consisted of nineteen men. Those I remember best were Ernst, who came from a farm in the Odenwald; Reinhard, a giant of a man from the Schwartzwald, who was told not to lean on a tank in case it fell over; Willy, who was small and sharp, with the cunning and assurance of a Hamburg alley cat; Hans and Kurt, who came from the Mosel valley; Alfred, from a small village in the Fränkische Schweiz; and lanky Walter, from Berlin.

From winter in France we came by ship to Tripoli. We

welcomed the fact that we were bound for North Africa, to what we thought was going to be an easy posting. We dreamed of the prospect of warmth and sun-splashed beaches, palm trees, swarthy, and we hoped compliant, maidens. There was much banter among the platoon about how many girls each one was going to collect. Willy had plans to set up a small hotel on the beach; Reinhard wanted to spend his time drinking cases of chilled beer; Ernst, Hans and Kurt would be content to laze on the beach with girls; Walter wanted what he called 'a bit of life', some snappy music, lots of girls, lots of dancing; Alfred was not interested in girls – he wanted to set up a little souvenir shop that would give him a tidy income, enable him to keep native servants ('Little boys, Alfred?' Willy asked) and live a life of ease.

'And you, Sergeant, what do you want?' Ernst asked.

I looked at their scrubbed, boyish faces, their close-cropped hair that made their necks seem so vulnerable. 'I want to live to be an old man,' I said.

'No girl will look at you then, Sergeant,' Walter said. 'I shall stay young for ever.'

We might almost have been going on a holiday. *Der Alte* soon changed all that, almost from the moment we disembarked. We set off at breakneck speed across the desert to Sirte, nearly 500 kilometres away, which we reached the next day. Here we remained for six weeks' training in desert warfare.

Within the first two days we forgot all about palm trees and beaches as all our training was inland on a constantly shifting landscape which consisted of sand, more sand and still more sand. The dry, stifling heat of the day fried us alive. Searing winds burned the face, scorched the tongue, cracked our lips and drove a fine powdery dust like millions of needles into the skin, burrowing into every crevice, covering vehicles and human beings alike. The sun plunged over the sandy horizon at 5.30 and the nights became freezing cold. The desert imposes its own refined torture in daily extremes of heat and cold. We longed for the stable winters of France and Germany.

The desert is a hostile, filthy place, where the elements conspire to reduce anything that moves to sand. With sunset flies appeared out of nowhere, swarming in battalions. They sucked our sweat, they covered our eyelids, our mouths, our nostrils, and as fast as we could shake them off, they settled again. As night deepened, myriads of sand fleas emerged and bit us all over until we felt like lumpy mattresses. Often we had no time to boil the water from the wadis and raging thirst forced us to drink what was available. Willy, Hans and Kurt were covered in blisters. Alfred and Walter had severe colic, and all of us retched frequently until we learned to endure thirst instead of drinking dirty water.

By the end of our six weeks we were leaner, dirtier, harder; we lived like desert animals. We learned how to move in the open desert like ships at sea, to navigate by the stars, compass and sextant. We learned how to make ourselves invisible, how to sit tight in sandstorms, how to live in and breathe and eat the sand until it became our natural element.

Our regiment was responsible for producing a secret weapon the like of which has never been seen in any army. This was what we christened the 'Cardboard Tank Division'. We had only 168 tanks in our whole division and the other division of the Afrika Korps was not due till April. *Der Alte* decided to take on the British with only half his total strength, knowing they had greater superiority in numbers and machines. We were ordered to round up as many Fiats as we could find which had been abandoned by the Italians in the desert around Tripoli. There were a hundred odd in all. We were ordered to turn them into 'tanks'.

'*Der Alte*'s gone off his rocker,' Willy said.

'He's asking the impossible,' Alfred said.

It was the Professor who decided how it should be done. He muttered something about a Trojan horse. He ordered us to fix a wooden chassis on each Fiat, cover it with canvas and screw on a dummy wooden tank gun. From a distance they looked indistinguishable from real tanks. They were moved at night, in small detachments, to Sirte.

Our first taste of fighting in North Africa was a relatively short one at El Agheila, three hundred kilometres east of Sirte. We moved at breakneck speed as usual. We attacked at night, using for the first time in an engagement the battle cry of the Afrika Korps: '*Heia Safari*!' Even I, hard-bitten, cynical, seasoned soldier that I am, even I felt my blood stir, my pulse race, as unit after unit charged into action with this war cry. '*Heia Safari*!' they shouted, and the shout was caught and echoed and re-echoed until the sand and sky rang with the call: '*Heia Safari*!' Such potent magic there is in the mere sound of words.

At dawn the British tanks were regrouping after withering anti-tank shelling. As they moved down the slopes towards us, we prepared to meet them head on. They saw on the distant horizon behind us, glinting in the first light of the sun, an armada of tanks coming straight towards them. They were our Cardboard Tank Division, which, together with our real tanks, outnumbered theirs. The British thought better of tangling with superior numbers, turned around and retreated eastwards. Our Cardboard Tank Division had won the day.

15

We seemed to be constantly on the move, pushing eastwards with very short, sometimes nonexistent, pauses between battles. The arrival of *der Alte* always meant pulling up stakes and moving on. He moved from unit to unit in his slow-flying Fieseler Storch aeroplane. I grew to recognize and hate the drone of its engines; it always meant trouble.

We had the luck of the devil until we captured Derna. We had been fighting continuously for ten days with very little sleep. Sometimes we dozed off in our positions without realizing it. Hans nearly got his head blown off on sentry duty. Had it not been for Kurt, from whom he was inseparable, he would have been our first casualty. Those two were like brothers despite the fact that they looked so different: Kurt dark-haired, dark-eyed, slow in speech; Hans very fair, his hair bleached white by the desert sun, his eyebrows so pale as to be almost invisible. We were low on fuel. Our tanks and lorries needed repairs. We were looking forward to a long rest at Derna. Instead we had to push on.

To Tobruk. This was a swine of a fortress. We were met by a ferocious artillery barrage. For the first time our infantry battalion was forced to withdraw southwards. We went in fighting formation, one group providing cover while another moved back, established a firing position, then signalled the first to move back under cover. We retreated to El Adem and safety. Here at least we could sleep without being fired on.

'Can't we return to Derna, Sergeant?' Alfred said. Alfred's nerves, never strong to begin with, had become increasingly shredded in the past few days; he jumped and shivered at the slightest sound.

'Our orders are to wait here. Get some sleep while you can.'

The men lay down with plenty of grumbles and fell asleep. If I had had my way, I'd not only have gone back to Derna but back to Tripoli and away from this bleeding, choking desert for good. But I was stuck here with them and there was no alternative. We all knew the attack on Tobruk had failed – our groaning wounded were testimony enough – but would *der Alte* admit it or ever be satisfied until he swallowed it whole? A man in love with war pursues victory with jealous eyes. I crushed a scarab beetle underfoot, cursed the desert and took a nap.

Two days later I was given my orders with all the other battalion NCOs. Another attack was planned. Tobruk's defences were concentrated on a twenty-kilometre-long anti-tank ditch that formed an arc round the fortress. Behind it were two hills used by the enemy as observation posts. Between the ditch and the hills were Australian troops, who had dug in with blockhouses and barbed wire.

The Armoured Pioneer Battalion, the Sappers, would be the first to go in. Their job was to cut the barbed wire, defuse the mines and open up paths for the rest of the division. We, the Infantry Battalion, were to cover the pioneers and then accompany 5 Panzer's tanks as they moved in. Each platoon was given its own path to follow. We would move with the leading tanks. Our front ranks, the assault force, would be the ones with grenades. The rest of the infantry would follow close behind them. The attack was to begin at midnight.

All through the day we watched the Australian positions which were nine hundred metres away. There was no movement. The desert looked empty. Sand dunes and sand and sun. The Australians too had learned to become invisible.

Alfred came to see me when I was on my own scanning the enemy lines. His face was white and he was clutching his stomach.

'I've got slashing pains in my stomach, Sergeant. I think it's my appendix.' He doubled up.

I made him lie down. 'When did this start?'

'It's been off and on for days now, Sergeant. I didn't say anything because we were busy. I'm afraid I'm not going to be much use in the attack tonight.'

Something in his voice made me suspicious. The explanation had come out a little too glibly, was too pat, as if rehearsed.

'You'd better rest here. I'll look in later.'

I returned an hour later. He was lying with his arm over his eyes.

'How are you, Alfred?'

'Worse if anything, Sergeant,' he said, screwing up his face.

'Where *is* the pain exactly?'

'Here,' he said, pointing to the wrong side.

'Get up, Alfred,' I said.

He did not move. I took my rifle, unlocked the safety catch and put it against his temple.

'You're lying, Alfred. I'll give you five seconds to get up. After that, this goes off.'

He did not move. 'I swear to you, Sergeant, I'm in great pain.'

'Five . . . four . . . three . . two . . .'

He sat up in one movement.

'I can't go into the attack, tonight, Sergeant. Please. I can't. Every time a gun fires I feel as if it's tearing me in two from head to foot. I'd be no good to you.'

'You'll go in with the rest of us, Alfred, or I'll blow your brains out.'

'Don't make me, please, I beg you.' He covered his face with his arm and wept like a child, his shoulders heaving in great sobs. 'I can't stand the guns. I can't, I can't.'

I put an arm around him and let him cry himself out. 'You stay with me when the attack begins, Alfred. You'll be all right. Better bathe your face before you join the others.'

My platoon cleaned and checked and counter-checked their rifles and machine guns. And then began the hardest part of the attack, waiting for it to begin. The desert night came on, black velvet, thick with stars. Reinhard was lying under the lorry that was to carry us.

'Sleeping still?' Ernst asked, peering underneath. He was

writing a letter home, sitting against one of the tyres, his broad face furrowed with concentration.

'Resting,' Reinhard grunted.

'Dreaming of girls,' Walter said, with a sly smile.

I passed around chocolate and water bottles. 'Better drink as much as you can. We won't have time later.'

'If we don't have time for a pee, Alfred will wet himself,' Willy said.

'And you, Willy?' asked Walter, his quizzical, good-humoured face tight with anger. 'What will you do? Shit in your pants?'

'Still playing nursemaid to him,' Willy said.

'Cut it out, both of you,' I said sharply. Our Berliner and our Hamburger never did get on and lately their tempers seemed to have got shorter.

Kurt and Hans were chatting quietly. The hours limped by. Somewhere in the darkness came the sound of 'Lorelei' played faintly on a mouth organ. Some of my men hummed it, some listened. Then Ernst began to sing softly in his pure, clear tenor the song that had become so familiar to us in the desert, broadcast every evening from Belgrade:

'Underneath the lantern, by the barrack gate,
Darling, I remember, how you used to wait.
It was there that you whispered tenderly,
That you loved me, you'd always be,
My Lili of the lamplight, my own Lili Marlene.'

Whenever I think of the desert and my time in it, that song and that voice come floating out of the past, redolent with memories: the desert night patterned with diamond stars, the smell of sand and fear, the sound of the young voices in my patrol: Ernst and Reinhard and Willy and Hans and Kurt and Alfred and Walter.

We sat in silence when the song had finished.

Alfred started and shivered. 'Listen!' he said.

We heard the faint rumble of 5 Panzer's tanks starting up. Then our own lorries started their engines.

The Professor appeared. 'Fall to.'

We lined up in platoons and piled into the lorries. At five minutes to midnight our lorry moved off northwards and stopped at the top of the hill in front of the enemy lines. No one spoke. Seconds ticked away. Twenty . . . fifteen . . . ten . . . five . . . Midnight – zero hour. With a tumult that tore the night sky into a thousand pieces, our artillery unloosed its barrage, the shells screaming over our heads as they arced and exploded over Tobruk. In that same moment our lorry raced down into the gully. We jumped out and lay flat against the barbed wire. The pioneers crawled forward, cut the wire, killed the mines. On and on they crawled, with us close behind them ready with covering fire.

At 12.15 all the guns suddenly stopped. The silence was deafening.

'Now! Forward!' the Professor said. We charged, ducking and weaving from one shell crater to another, machine guns covering each group. One group gave covering fire while the other one moved forward and established a position; then the first group moved forward covered by the second. Hans and Kurt, Ernst and Walter manned the two machine guns in our platoon; the rest of us carried grenades and rifles.

With a rumble and roar, 5 Panzer's tanks appeared like small, prehistoric monsters, devoured the barbed wire and anti-tank formations. We pushed forward covered by the tanks, grenaded the blockhouses and finished off the job with rifles. Then we waited while the tanks moved on again. This turn-and-turn-about formation was the way we advanced.

After ten hours we broke through at last to the anti-tank ditch. But the tanks were no longer with us. They had stopped five hundred metres behind us, pinned down by the Australian artillery. The pioneers began to fill in the anti-tank ditch; when the tanks arrived they would be able to move straight into Tobruk.

'Come on! Come on! Bring up your bloody tanks!' the Professor shouted.

We had cut the path through to Tobruk and were left without support. Two hours later four tanks arrived. Our battalion was under orders to keep the path constructed by the pioneers open at all costs. We held the place while another section attacked the Australians with the four tanks. By now the Australians had become aware of the breach in their defences and were paying us more attention. The four tanks ran out of ammunition and the attack failed. We learned later that in the process we had lost half our battalion. Alfred had disappeared. No one had seen him hit but there was no sign of him.

Five hours later and still our tanks had not moved. They seemed turned to stone. 'Don't fight like Italians,' Reinhard roared, shaking his fist at them. 'Take off your plimsoles!'

Suddenly British tanks appeared on the hills above us.

'Down! Down! Down!' the Professor shouted. We thought we were done for but they drove straight through our lines and attacked our tanks. About twenty tanks were knocked out and at last 5 Panzer moved – backwards. As they withdrew, the long-awaited Italian Division, which was supposed to support them at the outset, arrived and joined them as they retreated. Don't they have clocks in Italy? The Italians never seemed to arrive on time in the desert.

We were completely on our own now. What was left of our battalion was surrounded by the Australians. Night fell. We buried our dead under piles of stones. We could do nothing for our wounded; we left them at the anti-tank ditch to the mercy of the Australians. Behind us was a small hill that would give us greater shelter than our present position. An advance party from the battalion swept the Australians off it. We remained on that hill that night and for the next six days, dug into the sand like animals – without food, without water, without grenades, our ammunition perilously low. Somehow we had to get these if we were to survive. Reinhard cut a sleeping sentry's throat and brought us his water bottle and two bars of chocolate; he had the sense to take his rifle and ammunition as well. We raided enemy blockhouses at night and grabbed what we could of water, rations and weapons.

On the third day we saw an Italian division coming in our direction, we hoped on a rescue mission. At last, I thought, we'll be able to get away. But those bastards turned around and ran, ran as soon as the artillery opened up on them, leaving us high and dry. We ranged around that hill, digging for water and finding none.

On the fourth day an Australian officer lifted a white handkerchief tied to a rifle, stood up and shouted, 'Hey, we got plenty of water. You can have all you want if you surrender. You can't last out without it.' I would have taken his offer up immediately. We were surrounded, our tongues were swollen, our mouths cracked. But the battalion commander would not surrender. 'We shall wait,' he said.

That night Alfred appeared among us, crawling on all fours, crazy with sunstroke. He had tried to run away from the battlefield towards base, lost his way, and had been wandering around on the hill. Walter took charge of him, cradling his head like a baby. Reinhard killed another sentry and gave his share of the water to Alfred.

Two days later we were still there, scattered in little groups on that infernal hill. The Professor checked our ammunition. Our machine guns had no more belts left; our rifles were down to five rounds. The Professor was with our platoon that night when the Australians attacked. He ordered us not to fire until the enemy was well within our range. The firing from the battalion commander's position had ceased. We heard the Australians again shouting to him to surrender. In answer he and his men came charging out with fixed bayonets. They were mown down in seconds.

I looked at the Professor. Would he let us surrender? No such luck.

'At the ready,' he said.

Our rifles were lined up all along our trench, waiting for the enemy to come within our sights. I made up my mind what I would do once my rifle was empty. I certainly was not going to make an empty, heroic gesture rushing out with my bayonet into certain death. I would lie low and surrender.

I wasn't given the opportunity. While the battle raged all around us, no one approached our trench. By the goddamnedest hair's breadth of a chance, perhaps because we had dug our trench very deep, no Australians came to attack us. The Professor had sense enough not to hurl us into a suicide mission that would have achieved nothing. We stayed put over our rifles.

Next morning we saw the ground strewn with the bodies of our battalion. We stayed in our trench all day. That night the Professor took us back to our base at El Adem. There we discovered that we were all that was left of our battalion of 400 men.

16

That swine of a fortress became the graveyard for more men when we eventually took it the following year in June. War in Africa ended for me in November. My regiment had been outside El Alamein since the end of August. Attacks and counter-attacks, withdrawal and digging-in for a month, short of men, machines, weapons, fuel – it was Tobruk all over again, only this time what was left of the Africa Korps was there against an enemy that outnumbered us ten to one. 'Send us men and tanks, not buckets full of medals,' the Professor used to say, swearing at the High Command. But no replacements came for us – plenty of encouraging words, hot air that would have filled several gas balloons and cost nothing. Whole regiments were lost there in the big attack from the British at the end of October in ten days of the fiercest fighting I have ever seen.

We received the order to retreat. Tanks were filled quickly with diesel, artillery connected to carriers. A group of volunteers – Reinhard, Walter and Ernst among them – stockpiled grenades and machine guns to cover our retreat. Just as we were about to set out, *der Alte* countermanded his own order: 'On orders from higher authority, the present positions must be defended to the end.' Hitler and the desktop generals were meddling again. It was then that I got hit and plunged into darkness.

When I regained consciousness I found myself with the other wounded waiting for the lorry to take us to base hospital. Some could not wait that long and died. How simple death is on a battlefield. I heard the last words of those who slipped away around me – nothing profound or earth-shaking, no grand farewells or cinematic deathbed confessions, no agonies of remorse, no visions of glories to come. Merely:

'Tell my mother to bake the cake,' said the man on my right.

'I'll never make corporal now,' said the one next to him.

'I'll swim first; it's too hot to eat,' said another.

I was among the last of the wounded to be taken out of El Alamein. The Professor came to see me three times before I left. 'Are you comfortable, Martin? It won't be long now,' he said.

Not once did he mention his own predicament and that of the regiment, or what was left of it. In front of us were Montgomery's American Sherman tanks in a large crescent. Behind us, the enemy formations waiting in a semi circle, supplied daily with fresh men and machines.

The last time the Professor came, he said, '*Auf Wiedersehen*, Martin. You're lucky; you'll be out of this soon. If you get back to Germany, "Go, stranger, tell the Spartans that here we lie, having been obedient to their commands." '

By the time I reached the base hospital the whole regiment was wiped out. I saw them in my mind's eye, that ragged, rag-tag, bobtail group of men – Ernst, Reinhard, Willy, Hans, Kurt, Alfred, Walter, the Professor – and all the others of our regiment going at full speed with their patched-up, clapped-out remnants of five tanks, which was all we had left, straight into the jaws of death with the familiar battlecry ringing across the desert sands, shouting defiance at the enemy: '*Heia Safari*!'

I did not get back to Germany. I was moved to a hospital in Italy, where I had a long convalescence before being declared fit for active service again, this time in Yugoslavia.

17

By the summer of 1944 I had been in Yugoslavia just over a year. I had a new group of men, boys of eighteen who seemed younger than ever, since I was two years older and, at thirty-four, a sergeant still. They sat half dozing, some leaning back against the sides, some slumped over their rifles, cradling their heads in their arms, bumping along as our lorry moved in convoy along the dirt road. The heat shimmered in a haze along the limestone mountains pockmarked with caves and gullies. Patches of green were already scorching to brown in the open scrubland that stretched for kilometres against the mountains.

My unit had been on this road with similar convoys several times without trouble, but there was no certainty it would do so again. Any of the caves could be concealing bands of partisans. At any point the road could be booby-trapped. In this unpredictable country nothing could be guaranteed.

Three years ago, I was told by the old hands here, the Yugoslavs had provided ferocious opposition to the German army for ten days. Then, quite suddenly, they capitulated. Since then the population had been waging a war of attrition against the occupying German forces, using the mountainous terrain, which was ideally suited to guerrilla warfare, to their advantage. They emerged without warning, disappeared without trace. They fought the German army and they fought against their own people. The Ustasians, who were pro-German, fought against the Royalists, who supported the exiled king, and both groups fought the Communists led by Tito. It was a mad, savage country, light years removed from my green Sudeten valley, its lush meadows carpeted with flowers, trout leaping in the flashing river, and the sound of cowbells floating down the hillsides. There was also, of course, the widow Roth and the sound of Liese's scolding voice, but at a distance one remembers only the good things.

A shattering explosion brought the convoy to a halt. We jumped out quickly and took cover on the side of the lorry away from the hills. The leading lorry had gone over a mine, destroying the one behind it as well. The captain and an SS officer travelling with him to our headquarters were the only two left alive from the front lorries. The SS officer seemed dazed but unhurt; the captain was severely injured. 'Take charge, Sergeant,' he said, and passed out.

The ground behind us seemed empty but I placed one group of men to watch our rear. We were being shot at from the mountains. As long as we stayed behind the cover of our lorries we had shelter from the hail of bullets that came spattering from the high ground. There were bursts of rifle fire but the main damage was being done by a machine gun. It had to be destroyed quickly before it immobilised the whole convoy by shooting at the tyres.

I detailed three groups to advance at two-minute intervals towards the machine gun from the left, fanning out as widely as possible. They were to keep the enemy engaged. Simultaneously Private Langer and I, carrying grenades, would work our way to the machine gun from the right. I watched the men move out in short, quick bursts. The huge boulders that covered the hillside provided natural cover as they moved. If they scattered they would not make easy targets. For once the terrain could be used to *our* advantage.

As soon as the third group had left, Langer and I crawled out on our bellies, lying still whenever there was a lull in the firing, moving rapidly as soon as it broke out again. At last we were near enough to see the faces of the men operating the machine gun. We lay very still. At the next burst of firing we sent our grenades arcing through the air.

A shattering explosion. A sudden silence as the last of the debris floated down. Langer was shot through the head. A burst of firing from my men. Then silence again. No answering fire came from the mountains. The remaining snipers, if there were any, melted into the landscape.

I returned to the lorries to find that six of my men were dead. The captain had died also. The SS officer was unharmed. We resumed our journey and reached HQ without further incident.

Two days later I was summoned to the company major's room. The major was seated; the SS officer who had travelled with our convoy was standing by the major's desk. He was very tall and handsome, with a long, clean-cut face, neatly-parted hair and grey eyes that contradicted a mouth that smiled a lot. Everything about him exuded confidence and charm, from his gleaming black boots to his braided cap with the *Totenkopf* badge, the skull and crossbones, that he held in his hand. His black uniform fitted him as if it had been individually tailored.

'I've asked Major von Hassell to recommend you for the Iron Cross, Sergeant,' he said. 'I shall add a personal commendation.'

'Thank you, sir,' I said in my best military manner. He smiled while his grey eyes remained cold and appraising. 'I have also decided to recommend you for secondment to the SS.'

This was a bombshell, the last thing I wanted. The regular army despised the SS, whom they regarded as snoopers. They were Hitler's political army, moving freely among the regular army but not under its jurisdiction. Commissioned officers in the regular army came largely from aristocratic families with a long tradition of military service. The SS made a point of excluding the aristocracy from their ranks. They regarded themselves as an elite company drawn, like Hitler himself, from the common people. Now you would expect that I, being common as muck, would jump at the chance of joining the SS. In the army I would remain an NCO for ever; in the SS there was no limit to the rank I could aspire to. Yet I did not want to have anything to do with the SS. Why? Because I have never been a political animal. In my experience most of the horrors in the world have been caused in the name of religion or politics. And also because in Yugoslavia I had seen the SS in action as they killed hostages and exterminated whole villages in reprisal raids. I have no stomach for that kind of war. So I stood there silent, not knowing how to get out of this.

The SS officer smiled again indulgently. 'You don't say anything? It is a very high honour.'

'I don't think I'm worthy of such an honour, sir,' I said. Better butter the bastard up to hide my consternation.

'Good,' he said. 'You have the right attitude. The transfer will take place as soon as the paperwork goes through – a tedious but necessary formality. Congratulations.'

I came out with my head reeling. There was no way in which anyone could refuse to be taken into the SS. Once the summons came, it was as inevitable as death. I was the right height, the right build, the right colouring, and I had an unblotted army copybook. Whom did they have at their head, this elite political army? None other than the Reichsführer of the SS and chief of the German Police, Himmler, who was once a chicken farmer, a health faddist and nature bore. During the Depression he had 'gone back to nature', believing a man could only fulfil his destiny by living close to the soil, which was not to be contaminated by chemicals or artificial agents but fed by natural fertilisers only. Perhaps he fertilised his fields himself from his backside. And this crank's outfit was the one I had the 'honour' to be invited into.

That afternoon we were assembled for the usual lecture of political indoctrination that accompanied an SS man's visit to a regiment.

'I bring you,' said the SS officer, 'a personal message from Reichsführer Himmler: "Be brave, be strong, be eternally vigilant." The enemy outside is clearly identifiable; it will never triumph against the Fatherland. There is a more insidious enemy, the one within. Jews and Communists, who started this war, who fabricate lies about us abroad and perpetrate unspeakable acts at home, are the enemies of the German people. Their aim is the subversion of the nation from within, like woodlice burrowing into the structure of a building. Be vigilant, and their lies will always be found out. They destroy everything that National

Socialism seeks to achieve. What is the difference, I am often asked, between a Communist and a National Socialist? It is simple. Communism makes all men equal by dragging them down to the same level. National Socialism makes all men equal by lifting them *up* to the same level. There is a world of difference there. It is for this that we are fighting. It is for this that we shall continue to fight until victory is ours. "Be brave, be strong, be eternally vigilant." '

We put on our brave, strong and vigilant faces and were dismissed. Did he really believe the crap he spouted, I wondered, or was he just shooting a party line? They said so many things, these people who formed the charmed circle around Hitler. There was that monumental windbag Goering, who'd earned himself the title of Meier, a proper charlie, by boasting about the Luftwaffe. 'If a single British aircraft flies over Berlin,' he said, 'you can call me Meier.' That was four years ago and Berlin had been pounded by enemy bombers so often by now, that they had lost count. And now here was this arsehole explaining the difference between Communism and National Socialism. What *was* the difference? Both were dictatorships based on centralized power. Both controlled the media and relied on a state police and state judiciary. Both believed in eliminating all political opposition. One faced left, the other faced right, and, for all the claptrap about equality – levering people up or lowering people down – there would always be those who gave the orders, who grew fat and lived at ease, the generals and the commissars, and those who followed orders, the soldiers in the ranks and the common people who would always have someone above them pulling them up or down or sideways or any which way.

The next day I was summoned again to the major's room. The SS officer stood at the same place but there was no welcoming smile. The face was stern, the eyes hard.

'Sergeant Bron,' he said, 'how do you spell your name?'

'M A R T I N, sir.'

'Your surname,' he said icily.

'B R O N, sir.'

'Have you always spelled it this way?'

'Yes, sir.'

'I have made a special study of names, Sergeant. Do you know why?'

'No, sir.'

'It's quite simple. To discover infiltrators and imposters.'

I waited silently, not having any idea what he was on about. Perhaps it was some kind of test for the SS.

' "Bronn", Sergeant, with two "n"s is a good German name. "Bron" with one "n" is an abbreviation of a Jewish name, "Bronstein". Am I getting through, Sergeant?'

'Sir?'

'It is no use playing the innocent. Your name shows you are a Jew."

'I'm a Catholic, sir.'

'So your army record says. The SS investigation will go into the matter thoroughly. Where were you born?'

'In Teschen, in Austria.'

'Teschen is part of Poland,' he said, not caring to hide the note of triumph in his voice.

'Everyone knows I'm a Catholic, sir. I have nothing to hide.'

'I am glad you think so. We shall find proof, one way or another. In the meantime, the recommendation for the Iron Cross will, of course, be cancelled.'

Major von Hassell got up. 'I'm afraid that will not be possible. The request has already gone to Army HQ.'

'Then cancel it.'

'I'm sorry, but I can't,' the major said. 'You yourself were a witness to what happened. A recommendation for valour cannot be withdrawn.'

'The Iron Cross can never be worn by a Jew.'

'Nor can it be taken away, once given – *never* in the regular army.'

'Very well.' He turned on his heel and marched out.

The major sat down again and ran his hands through his hair. 'He's leaving us tomorrow. You're married, aren't you, Sergeant, with children?'

'Yes, sir. Three.'

'The SS will investigate your wife and chilren as well. It would be a good idea to write to your wife so that she is not alarmed by their appearance. I'm sure it will all come to nothing.'

But I wasn't so sure. For the first time after so many years I felt acutely conscious of my Jewish origins. I remembered my mother's words: 'Once a Jew, always a Jew. You can never be anything else.' But I *had* become something else and I was not going to change my chameleon existence now. What crimes had the Jews committed to be branded at birth? My parents, and the other Jews I had known until I came to Waldburg were no better and no worse than the Catholics I had known since I settled there.

I had to warn Liese immediately but it would be as dangerous writing to her as not informing her. With her insistence on truth at all costs, she would believe she was safe if she told the SS the truth. She was incapable of realizing that she would condemn me, herself and the children by her honesty. Since all mail was censored, I could not write openly to her and instruct her to act as I advised. Even if there were no censorship, she would still not do as I asked; she would rely on her moral code, which was inflexible. There is nothing more exasperating or dangerous than a good woman who remains good at all costs.

The only person who could make her see the danger was Father Klein. She would listen to him; she would follow his advice; she would follow him to the gates of hell if he asked her. Once again, at a time of dire necessity, this priest whom I disliked intensely was the only one I could turn to. And this made me dislike him even more. When Heinrich had come wounded to our flat, it was Father Klein who had helped us out. When Katzer and his friends had beaten me up, Father Klein had seen to it that they became objects of shame for the whole town. Now, once again, I had to rely on him completely. I did not want to have anything to do with him or his Church, but I could never be free of him. And the maddening part of it all was that he never forced himself on me. *I* was forced to go to him, time after time.

I wrote to him immediately, stating that I was being seconded to the SS and, as soon as the paperwork was over, would be transferred from the regular army. I asked him to pass this news on to Liese and make sure she understood the difference it would make in my status. He was intelligent enough to understand the implications and act accordingly.

The SS would ferret out what they could. And yet what proof could they get their hands on? I did not have my birth certificate; I had no idea whether my parents had it either. I did not know where my parents were. Their wandering existence was now my strongest safeguard. If I had been born a Catholic, my birth would have been recorded in a church register at baptism. Teschen would be extensively damaged in bombing raids by now. I could not possibly be expected to know in which church precisely I had been baptized as an infant when my parents were passing through. The absence of records would be in my favour.

But my adult baptism was recorded in the church in Waldburg. If that was discovered I would be *kaput* – finished. I did not know whether my parents were alive or dead. Had they fled to safety or been caught? I had lost touch with them completely. My father had written at long intervals, but when the war started the letters stopped. I should have replied. I should have written. I felt a sudden rush of pity for my parents: my submissive, henpecked father, my wearisome, demanding mother, whom I saw now in one of her rare, uncritical moments. I must have been a trial to her – a difficult, mischievous child, always drawn towards the forbidden, the unusual, the unconventional. They must be old now, but I could only visualize them as I had last seen them. I hoped they had fled the country, as much for their sake as mine.

18

Much later I learned from Father Klein what he had done. First of all he extracted the relevant church register with several others and hid them. He rearranged the remaining registers to form a continuous line on the shelves.

'The church and presbytery were redecorated just before the war,' he said. 'You've no idea how many objects were lost or misplaced at the time. Some of them turned up months later; some, I'm afraid (your register among them), disappeared altogether.'

Then he journeyed all the way to Teschen to see the bishop. The whole of the Polish area of Teschen had been bombed repeatedly, churches and synagogues reduced to rubble. It would be impossible to find any records, Catholic or Jewish, there. With the bishop's help he had managed to trace my parents. They had died in 1942 in a camp called Auschwitz. There was no record of their having any children. You must realize that at that time Auschwitz, Buchenwald and Treblinka were mere names to me, places that I thought were labour camps. Since traffic was all one way into those places during the war, there was no hint of what took place inside. As news was state-controlled, the 'men' who ran those charnel houses, usually the SS, had no need to talk about what they were doing; and the dead certainly never walked out. I suppose the people who built the ovens had no way of knowing what they were built for. With hindsight it seems incredible, but, at the time, could anyone have imagined such a monstrous purpose for them? The secret was kept – as completely as that of the Czech concentration camps after the war, which most people do not even know existed.

Father Klein had risked his life for me by going to Teschen. If the SS tied him to me or discovered his visit, he would be done for. This small, slight priest with his lined face and gentle eyes had no thought of himself at all. I admired his courage but I disliked him more than ever. What right had he to put his own life on the line for me? I hadn't asked him to do so. I would have been content with what he had done to his own church registers. I was more than content at the way in which he had advised Liese over the whole business. Why did he have to spoil it all by excess? He never knew where to draw the line. He had to give everything, withholding nothing of himself. I did not want it. I felt stifled. It was to my advantage but I did not want it this way, from this man of all men.

The SS investigation was over. I was told by the major that they had found no documentary proof, but because I could not provide papers to clear myself I was to be dismissed from the army. The major was angry and apologetic. He had tried to get my dismissal revoked, but the SS had more pull in certain quarters. He gave me a personal reference for whoever became my future employer. I offered to return the Iron Cross but he insisted I keep it. He was an easy man to work for, in spite of his aristocratic background. He asked me not to tell my platoon I'd been discharged since it might demoralize them. I never saw him again and have no idea whether he survived the war.

So I was homeward bound, kicked out of the army I had served in for five years, at a time when the country needed every available man in its fight for survival. Boys of sixteen and old men of sixty were being roped in as soldiers. Everyone knew by now that we would lose the war. I think we knew the war had turned against us when Stalingrad was lost early in the previous year. The whole of the German 6th Army perished there, just as the whole of the Afrika Korps had perished in the months after El Alamein. The reason was the same: Hitler's refusal to allow his generals to withdraw their troops to safe positions in order to fight another day. The order from Hitler and the High Command was 'Stand and fight.' They stood – and died.

Daylight bombing raids and round-the-clock bombing of German cities were by now commonplace. The bombers certainly destroyed communications and therefore brought about defeat, because, although the factories were working full blast, it was impossible to transport weaponry components or the finished product by road or rail. Shells in one place, guns in another, and no way the two could meet. No one knew whether fuel was actually in short supply or simply could not be transported to planes and lorries. The bombing of centres of industry, communication and military targets was to be expected. But I have never been able to understand the reason why cities which had nothing in them except civilians were marked out by the British and Americans for round-the-clock bombing that reduced them to rubble. Cologne, Würzburg, Nuremberg among others, and early in the following year the most incomprehensible of all, Dresden: a city into which thousands of refugees had poured from the surrounding areas, and where more civilians were killed than by the combined bombs of Hiroshima and Nagasaki.

Times were hard in Waldburg but we were better off than in the cities. Food was rationed but, although everyone grumbled, we got by. In the summer there were berries; in the autumn there were nuts and the countryside provided a variety of plans and fungi for unusual but quite edible soups. We burned wood because fuel was scarce. Most important of all, Waldburg and the surrounding areas were spared all bombing. Death here crept slyly in through the letter box.

I caught up with news of friends and relatives. Liese's brother had suffered the terrible Russian winter of 1941: his regiment was dressed in summer clothing; machine guns seized up and fuel froze; the only way they could start their tanks was by lighting fires underneath them, and the army lost twice as many men from frostbite as from enemy fire. Hitler commanded them to dig in where they were, out in the open, forbade them to withdraw to sheltered positions. Her brother had survived that ordeal by frost only to be killed at Stalingrad.

Max had been wounded, lost a lung and was invalided out of the army. He was posted to Berlin where he was working in a plant making synthetic petrol. Friedrich was last heard of fighting on the Russian front. Gerhard was in Hungary as an interpreter on the staff of the German general in Budapest.

I was posted to the timber mill at Auernig about ninety kilometres to the east, to supervise Russian prisoners-of-war who were brought there daily from their camp. They loaded timber onto carts drawn by huge drayhorses. I was warned to keep my eyes open; one of the prisoners had escaped after killing the guard whose place I now took.

I watched them closely, these men: haggard, dirty, unshaven, with a grey pallor in their faces and hunger in their eyes – my enemies, who would, given half a chance, have cut my throat. The enemy. Across the barrel of a gun, dug into trenches, in battle, the term had some meaning. But here it was meaningless. Had the fortunes of war gone the other way, we could have changed places. These men were down on their luck. For all that, I would not turn my back on them.

They brought their midday rations with them and ate them quickly from cupped hands, bolting the food like animals. On one occasion a man dropped a piece of bread on the ground. He fell upon it, scooped it up and pushed it into his mouth, earth, sawdust and all, before the others were aware that it had left his hands.

In the first week I was there one of them was bending over a log, heaving it without managing to shift it. I walked over to him and stopped just behind him. As soon as the man became aware of my presence he stood up and turned round flinching, one arm drawn across his face.

'What's the matter?' I asked.

He stood there, his eyes full of fear and hate.

I raised my arm to point to another prisoner and the man flinched again. He expected me to hit him. Perhaps the guard I had replaced had lashed out at them so often that they expected it from me as well.

I stepped back from him, pointed to another prisoner and said, 'Help him to lift this log. It's too heavy for one man.'

With the onset of winter familiar faces disappeared among the POWs and were replaced by new prisoners at regular intervals. The winter proved too harsh also for an old drayhorse, who lay down and died. He should have been carted off to the glue factory, but I asked the owner if I could cut him up and give him to the prisoners, who were starving.

'Feeding prisoners is not our responsibility,' he said. 'The camp arranges for their food.'

'If we feed them our production figures will rise,' I said. 'They'll be able to do double the amount of work they do now.'

He agreed and the stench of boiling horse filled the air. The POWs gorged themselves that day and secreted what they could in their pockets. At the rate some of them ate, I thought they would burst their stomachs. I'm sure the horse, given the choice, would have preferred to be eaten than turned into glue.

Part Three Phoenix Burning

19

The cold spring of 1945 brought the sound of guns, like distant thunder, closer every day. Breslau, one of the German fortresses to be defended to the last man, was only seventy-five kilometres away.

One morning no prisoners arrived at the timber mill. 'The Russians are coming.' The cry ran like a forest fire through Auernig. The German army was urging the civilian population to move out to safety.

I went to the stables, hitched up two drayhorses to a cart and drove to the centre of the town. Liese was not around to harangue me for stealing my transport. No point in leaving those patient, beautiful animals for the Russians. They might eat them. I needed them now, their strength, their willingness to pull and carry and serve with a dignity unmatched by the men who use them. Of all animals, the horse is the noblest, and these two, with their velvet flanks and bushy feet, their large liquid eyes and weather-vane ears, among the best.

All the shops in the town were thrown open. 'Take what you want,' the shopkeepers said. 'The Russians are coming.' I helped myself to food, matches and clothes and drove as fast as the horses could carry me to Waldburg.

The children immediately started quarrelling over who was to look after the horses. Leo and Erika, who were eleven and ten years old now, adopted one each; little Dietrich, who was seven, had to be content with doing odd jobs for both of them as a mark of great favour.

'Pack what you can and load it onto the cart. We're moving out,' I said to Liese. 'It won't be long before this town becomes a battle zone. If they shell the town before moving in, they'll reduce it to rubble.'

Liese had on her stubborn face, which always spelled trouble.

'I'm not moving from my house. Even if the Russians come, they can't kill us. We can't just up and go, like gypsies. There's nowhere for us to go. I was born here. My family's here. All my relations are here.'

'If we stay we'll all be killed. Have you any idea what a bombardment of a town is like? The Russians have broken through along the entire eastern sector. They'll be here any day. We may have as much as a week, as little as two days. We *have* to get out. We've no choice.'

'Our army will stop them.'

'Our army is finished, *kaput*,' I shouted. 'We have boys of sixteen trying to be soldiers – without training, without equipment. Can't you see they can't perform miracles?'

'Perhaps we shall get a miracle. We must not lose faith. I shall light a candle to the Virgin.'

I felt like taking her by the shoulders and shaking some sense into her. 'Light a whole boxful of candles, light the whole church up if you want. Perhaps if you burned it down, you wouldn't talk such nonsense. You've got religious mania. God isn't going to stop the Russian army – they don't believe in him – not unless he drops tanks on them from the sky.'

'You are the seed that was thrown on stony gound,' she said. 'Your faith was always shallow. I'm putting my trust in God. He's never failed me yet.'

I was so angry I could have hit her for such stupidity. I picked up the kitchen chair I was leaning on and smashed it onto the ground.

'*Gott im Himmel*! What am I to do to make you see sense? You're insane. Very well. You can stay with God and the Russians, since you have such faith in them. I'm leaving tomorrow, and I'm taking the children with me.'

I stormed out and went to the *Gasthaus* to cool down with several beers. Women! Bloody, stupid women! There really was no cure for stupidity. Goodness, stupidity, piety – each on its own is difficult enough to handle. I had the lot in one bundle. For the first time I understood my father; he had opted for a quiet life in the only way he knew how: by allowing himself to be henpecked. Did Crippin carve up his wife for the same reason? Had matters come to such a head that he had either to chop her up or to hang himself? He ended up doing both. She had the last word, after all.

I made my slightly unsteady way to Max's parents. Max seemed to be managing reasonably well on his one lung in Berlin. I offered them a place in the cart. To my astonishment they refused.

'My whole life has gone into the bakery and this house,' Max's father said. 'I won't leave them for the Russians or anyone else. If they kill me, they kill me. At least I'll die in my own home. No blasted Russian is going to drive me out of it.' His bald, round head gleamed like a billiard ball in a shaft of sunlight. His broad, strong hands, the fingernails whitened by flour, clasped his knees in an attitude of entrenched defiance. 'The Russians need to eat, like anyone else. Unless they have bakers with them, they'll leave me alone.'

Nothing I said would make him change his mind. His wife and grown-up daughters refused to go without him.

'When Max leaves Berlin,' his wife said, 'he will come home. We must be here when he comes back.'

They seemed to have a death wish and I could do nothing about it.

I went to Liese's parents. There was no love lost between her mother and me although I got along very well with her father. His nose, which had always been the most colourful feature in his face, was now plum red. He had grown a beer belly and moved with difficulty. Never a garrulous man (it was difficult to put in a word edgeways with his wife around), he had grown almost silent after his son's death at Stalingrad.

I asked them to persuade Liese to go with me. I did not fancy looking after three children on my own. It is woman's work and I no more expected to do it than I wanted to send Liese out to chop firewood or earn a living to support the family. For the first and only time in her life, Liese's mother agreed with me. So did her father. In fact, both of them assumed that I would be taking them with me. I had not bargained on this. It was difficult to know which was worse: leaving Liese behind on her own or having her and her mother with me. The combination of Liese and her mother was enough to drive a man into a permanent alcoholic haze. I was sorry I had come and left hurriedly with as much good grace as I could muster.

I walked about to clear my head and found my steps leading me to Friedrich's door. Martha received me stiffly with the cold politeness reserved for a stranger. I asked for news of Friedrich.

'There was a letter from him from the Russian front – where that is is anyone's guess – two months ago. As far as I know, he's still there.'

I told her Waldburg would be evacuated of civilians soon, that she should leave as quickly as possible.

'Have you any relatives you can go to? The children should be taken to a safer place.'

'I have an aunt in Erzbach,' she said. 'It's a small village in the hills but it's very far from here. There are no trains now; it would take us weeks to get there on foot. I don't think the children could make it. We'll be better off here.'

'I have a cart and two drayhorses. We're leaving tomorrow. You can come with us.'

'Thank you,' she said proudly, 'but I think we'll stay here and hope for the best.'

'If you change your mind, my offer still stands. A battle zone is no place for children.'

I left her standing with her arms folded across her chest, lips set, her square, stocky figure firmly planted. Her face, which had once been pretty, was lined and heavy, her hands rough and red with work.

I felt she regarded changing her mind as a sign of weakness. She was proud of being independent, of managing; she never liked taking help from others; it left her beholden to them and she felt burdened until she had returned the favour in some way. Would she value her pride and fierce independence above the safety of her children? On the rare occasions when I had met her in the old days she had never disguised her dislike of me in words of frozen politeness with a look that would curdle milk. She always linked me with the loss of Friedrich's business and behaved as if the Jew who swindled him was my brother.

I thought of Friedrich, with his slow smile and quiet, considerate ways, and Martha, with her starched pride and readiness to take offence where none was meant. What kind of a life had he led with her? He had seemed happy enough and certainly never complained. But he was never given to complaining, even in the hard times. His violin and his music gave him a self-sufficiency of spirit although he had so little in the way of worldly goods. It was a strange match, what psychologists nowadays would call 'temperamental incompatability', if you could afford their fees, and divorce lawyers call 'mental cruelty', while totting up their astronomical charges which would burn a far crueller hole in their clients' pockets. And yet perhaps it was not really so strange. No stranger certainly than my own marriage. Could it be that Martha reserved an unsuspected part of her character for the privacy of her home, a part which was never revealed to the world outside? Could it be that her husband and children saw in her a sweetness all the richer for being hoarded in so miserly a fashion? Or was it Friedrich's accommodating nature that had adapted itself to her prickly personality? Friedrich, who bent like a willow under whatever burdens life heaped on him and raised his head again with a calm inner strength that withstood all? Where was he now? No heroics, no fuss, total reliability – that had always been Friedrich's way, pursued with quiet, unspectacular courage. He was, for me, the brother I never had.

When I got home Liese was packing. She would not stay without her parents. I had jumped once again from the frying pan into the fire.

20

'The Russians are coming! The Russians are coming!' People were rushing all over the place. Shops were thrown open, abandoned by their owners. Everyone took what they wanted. Some barricaded themselves in their homes; others packed what they could in bundles, suitcases, boxes, piled them onto wheelbarrows and prams and poured out of the town westwards. The majority were on foot, carrying enormous loads which they had to discard along the way.

I was loading the cart when Martha and her two children arrived. She made the children stand near a battered suitcase some distance away and came forward alone. She stood with her feet apart as if on the deck of a rolling steamer.

'Please . . . please . . .' She clenched her fists and smote her breast several times. '*Mein Gott! Mein Gott!* I never thought . . . I never knew . . . I am alone. The children . . . You must take the children. You can leave me here but take them. For Friedrich's sake. I'm sorry . . . I didn't mean . . . Please.'

'Come inside, Martha. Of course I'll take the children *and* you.'

In the living room she sat down heavily, burst into tears and blew her nose loudly, angry at her own weakness.

'Your wife won't mind our coming with you?'

'Of course not. Why should she?'

She did not answer but gave a huge shrug of her shoulders as if to say, who can tell?'

'Do you want to go to your aunt's?'

'Yes, in Erzbach. What will you charge for taking us?'

I looked at her in amazement.

'I have what's left of Friedrich's army money,' she said, 'but it's not much. I've kept the clothes my children have outgrown – they're quite clean, they should fit Leo and Erika.'

'I can't take payment from you, Martha. Friedrich would have done the same for Liese and our children if he'd been in my place.'

She flushed guiltily. Perhaps she knew that she would have tried her utmost to prevent Friedrich from doing so.

'You *must* take the clothes. I've nothing else to give you. Please, you must.'

There was a look of desperation on her face. I felt that if I refused payment she might once again decide not to come with us.

'Very well. The clothes will be most useful.'

'Where are you going? Have you relatives to go to?'

'No, we'll stay wherever we find a place to take us.'

'You can stay at my aunt's. I'm sure she'll put you up.'

'Liese's parents are coming with us. There may not be room for all of us.'

'I'll ask her to make room,' she said firmly. 'I still have food in the house, and my clothes.'

'Leave your suitcase here. Go home, pack what you want and I'll come and pick you up as soon as I've collected Liese's parents.'

'Can I bring our eiderdowns?' she said, looking at ours piled on the cart.

'Yes, and anything else you need.'

'What about the children?'

'They can stay here.'

Liese came in from the kitchen. The two women greeted each other awkwardly. Liese had not forgotten Martha's attitude towards me when Friedrich's business collapsed, and although she felt she had a licence to censure me for everything I did, she took it as a personal affront when anyone outside the family ciriticized me. So the air suddenly became icy.

'Martha and the children are coming with us,' I said.

'Oh?' She managed to convey in that single syllable surprise, disapproval and insult, tempered with heavy Christian forbearance.

Martha bristled. 'I'll go home and pack,' she said. She was at the door when she stopped, her face white with apprehension. 'You *will* come for me? You won't leave me behind?'

Her independence seemed to have made her incapable of trusting anyone. Before Liese could give a tart reply, I said, 'Of course I'll come. Look, if it makes you feel safer, take Franz and Maria with you and I'll pick you all up together. Or do you think I'll leave the children behind as well?'

'No, no, of course not. I'm a stupid woman. I'll leave the children here.'

She bustled off, a square, stocky figure on short, sturdy legs.

We collected Liese's parents and found Martha waiting at her front door, her belongings stacked neatly beside her.

'I've been so worried,' she said. 'I sat near the window but I couldn't sit still. I walked up and down. Twice I heard horses' hooves and rushed to the door, only to find it wasn't you. Thank God you've come.'

As we drove through the town a figure suddenly darted into the middle of the road and stood with arms outstretched. I pulled the horses up sharply, shouting, '*Himmelkreuz und Donnerwetter!* You bloody fool! Find some place else to commit suicide.'

The horses stopped within a few inches of the figure. It was the widow Roth, bobbing and smiling from the slit in her putty-like face.

'Herr Bron! Herr Bron!' she said, flapping her arms about like a ragged cow. 'You are a good Catholic. I've always said so. For the love of Christ, take me with you.'

'God strike her dead for being such a hypocrite,' Martha said.

'Wherever you're going, take me with you. Out of this town. I have no one to turn to, Herr Bron. You are a good man. Please, for

Christian charity, take me with you. I can't stay here alone. I'm frightened.'

I was about to drive on when she said, 'Father Klein said I could take his place.'

'I didn't offer him a place.'

'I did,' Liese said, 'but he wouldn't come. He said his place was here, with his people, and no one would harm a priest.'

'He had no right to send someone else.' I was angry at his interference, his assumption that any substitute he sent would be acceptable to me.

'He had every right,' Liese said. 'We can just about fit you in, Frau Roth.'

'Will you wait a moment for me, please?' Without waiting for an answer, she ran into her house and came out clutching an expensive suitcase. She clambered into the cart. 'You are a saint, Herr Bron. God will reward you for this.'

I have always found that those who believe they sit on God's right hand are the most untrustworthy. I scowled at her, swore under my breath and urged the horses on. Frau Roth settled herself comfortably, sitting primly upright, her hands clasped on her lap, a simpering smile on her face, looking about her graciously as if she were riding in a chauffer-driven limousine.

'We're quite full, aren't we? We shan't be able to take on anyone else. We have to draw the line somewhere.'

Liese's parents looked at her with distaste. Martha glared at her with such unadulterated venom that anyone less thick-skinned would have withered with shame. She sat oblivious of everything except her own importance. I felt like pushing her out of the cart. I couldn't stand the woman. She is the only person I know who looks worse when she smiles. She had never forgotten my Jewish origins, never failed to point to them and draw disparaging conclusions when discussing me with her friends at her weekly coffee parties. She regarded Liese and her family as having brought disgrace on the German people by forming an alliance with someone who could never become wholly respectable. Liese had told me of this and resented it, but if Father Klein had offered his place to the devil, she would have taken him in. Religion, once again rearing its ugly head, interfering with our lives and our judgement and, as you will see later, bringing needless calamities on our heads. I cursed him roundly and wished to God Father Klein would get out of my life for ever.

21

We travelled for two days, camping out in the woods at night close to the cart and horses. The village of Erzbach, a straggle of houses and outlying farms, was already full of refugees. Martha's aunt's cottage turned out to be derelict – plaster was peeling off the walls, the roof timbers sagged, the whole building bent under the weight of dirt, decay and neglect.

Martha went to the door and shouted, 'Tante Maria! Tante Maria!'

Barefoot, ragged children appeared, stared at us and vanished, calling for their mother. More children emerged and stood gawping at us. A slatternly woman with long, dark hair and sharp features followed, shouted at the children, then shouted at us.

'What do you want?'

'My aunt, Maria Schuster lives here, doesn't she?'

'I live here with my children. There was no one here when I moved in.'

'She can't have moved. We've come to stay with her.'

'There is no one else here. There never was. Come in and see for yourself.'

Martha followed her in. I wondered whether she thought her aunt was being held captive in a cupboard or whether natural curiosity made her go in. She returned, her face crinkled with disgust.

'The place is a pigsty. It stinks. I had a good look round. My aunt would never keep it in this condition.'

The widow Roth sat with her handkerchief over her mouth as if the very air was contaminated for someone with her sensibilities.

'You've brought us all this way for nothing,' she said. 'Where can we go now?'

'Nobody asked you to come,' Martha said.

'We'll see if a farmer will take us in,' I said. 'He might want workers.'

'I don't think I'm really fitted for farm labour,' the widow objected.

'You weren't really fitted for riding in a cart,' I snapped, 'but you've managed well enough. I can drop you off in the village instead. I'm sure you'll fit in there.'

'Oh no, I'll stay with you. We must stick together.'

Like a leech, I thought, and drove on.

The first two farms we stopped at had no rooms to spare. At the next one the farmer took his time before he gave an answer. He was a small thin man in his sixties, his back slightly bent; bushy white eyebrows formed an umbrella over shrewd grey eyes that appraised us.

'I might be able to use a couple of farm hands,' he said. 'But I can't pay you,' he added quickly. 'You can have food and a room, but it's not big enough for all of you.'

He walked round the cart, looked carefully at the horses, who stood patient and docile, their flanks glowing with sweat. He rubbed his hand up and down their necks, patted their velvet noses and said, 'These seem to be fine animals,' his sharp eyes darting a quick acquisitive glance at me.

'They're not for sale. But if you take us in I could loan them to you for work on the farm.'

With a great show of reluctance he said, 'I'll take your family and your in-laws but the others will have to go to the school; the Bürgermeister is taking refugee women and children in the school hall.'

Our room was large and bare, situated just under the loft. It had been used as a storeroom and smelled of rye and hay. Piles of sacks were stored in a corner. I left Liese and her mother busy making the room habitable. On the floor below ours there was a small room, about the size of a cupboard, with a stone sink where we could wash. The other occupants of the house were the farmer's wife – a buxom woman with a dour face – and two plain daughters with the quiet, patient look of spinsters who were resigned to their fate.

I went outside to find Martha sitting under a tree some distance from the cart, with her back to it in an attitude of quivering indignation. The widow Roth sat in state on her suitcase in the cart, looking like offended royalty.

'That woman!' Martha said. 'That wicked, ungrateful, hypocritical, spiteful woman! You should never have brought her with you.'

I am not interested in women's quarrels; nine times out of ten they are about trifles blown up into mountains. I did not ask for an explanation but Martha gave me one none the less.

'She's been saying all kinds of things behind your back. She's been making a long string of complaints: about the journey, about going to my aunt's, about you. "We've been left to fend for ourselves," she said. "We don't know anyone here." "Neither do the Brons," I said. "You heard the farmer; there just isn't room." "Oh, I know what he *said*," she answered. "If Herr Bron had refused to loan him the horses unless he housed all of us, he'd have agreed straightaway." "Then no one would have been taken in," I said. "Martin's not in a position to strike bargains." Do you know what she said then? "It's only to be expected. It's a well-known Jewish characteristic. They only look after their own, no matter how much we do for them. It's small wonder they're universally disliked." "I don't know what *you've* ever done for him," I said, "except talk behind his back." And with that I left the cart and came here.'

'Sticks and stones, Martha,' I said, and took them, sitting in opposite corners of the cart, to the school, Martha making her children sit with their backs to the widow as well.

'I'll never forget what you've done for us, Martin,' Martha said.

'You know where we are. If you need anything, just come and ask.'

But would she, I wondered, as I drove back to the farm, she who resented having to ask anyone for anything, who relied so much on herself that she had made independence into one of the seven deadly virtues? She had built a wall around herself like a castle standing defiantly against the surrounding countryside: quite formidable but, I think at times, very lonely too.

22

Work on the farm was hard but we never went short of food: milk, butter, eggs, bread which the farmer's wife baked in weekly batches in the outdoor oven, and when a pig was killed, a thick nourishing soup made from scraps and trotters. I found living with six other people in one room more irksome than labouring on the farm. The children adapted more easily than the rest of us. Their only anxiety when we arrived was the absence of a flush toilet. The farmer had a lean-to shed, without running water, next to the chicken house, used exclusively by his family. 'In the summer,' he said, 'I don't use the shed at all. There's plenty of space in the woods and fields. It's good for the soil.' He gave me permission to build a small hut well away from the house, where I made a raised seat with a hole in it, placing a pile of clean straw underneath – primitive but better than a bush or a tree for the womenfolk. The children hated it. Dietrich cried and screamed, 'I'll fall down the hole, I'll fall, I'll fall. It's a long way down.'

At the end of April news came over the wireless: 'Our beloved Führer has been killed in action in Berlin defending the Fatherland.' We did not know till much later that he blew his brains out. Or so they say. For all I know, he may, like a number of other important men who vanished, be living a life of ease in South America with a new name, a new face, a new passport, dreaming of new worlds to conquer. Politicians have a knack of living in luxury while the world burns around them.

The news could only mean that the end of the war was imminent. Perhaps now, at last, I thought, those who wanted to negotiate terms with the Americans could do so and the Russians might still be prevented from overruning the country. Now, as I'm scribbling away here with my own world shot down in flames, I recall a broadcast by Dr Goebbels during the war: 'If the German people were to lay down their arms, the Soviets will occupy the whole of Eastern and Southeastern Europe, plus the largest part of the Reich. In front of these territories an iron curtain will at once come down, behind which the mass slaughter of the people will take place . . . Europe's political bourgeoisie is so frightened of death that it is committing suicide by allying itself out of hate and despair with a revolutionary power that cannot win without its help but which will choose a suitable moment after victory to do away with the people who have made victory possible.' We who heard him then thought this was mere propaganda, and yet how strangely prophetic his words turned out. And the fat Englishman with the cigar, around whom Stalin ran smoke rings, made the world believe after the war that *he* had discovered 'the iron curtain' he stole from Hitler's Minister of Propaganda. Now, I have often told, and still tell, lies, but never, I think, such a whopper. The only difference between the Engländer and me in this respect is that he gets showered with honours for telling them while I get sour looks and harangues from Liese.

Within a few days the war ended – no negotiations, no discussions, no gestures even of 'peace with honour'; total, abject, unconditional surrender – *kaput!* Even though I had seen it coming for a long time, knew there was no way in which it could be avoided, prided myself on my realism while Liese prayed for a miracle, in spite of it all, the defeat of my country came as a cruel blow. I thought of the men I had served with and the fresh-faced boys whom this war swallowed in convulsive gulps, their slate wiped clean before they ever had a chance to write on it. The dead rose up around me and moved about the room in a long, long line. I heard their voices, their laughter, their banter, their curses. I heard the sound of their marching feet and their songs: many bawdy, some martial, some piercingly sweet. I smelt their tobacco and their sweat and felt the power and beauty of young men at the beginning of the world. I thought of Friedrich in Russia, Max in

Berlin, Gerhard in Hungary. Were they still alive or rotting in a ditch, eaten by maggots?

The Russians arrived. Marauding bands of soldiers from a nearby town, where they were garrisoned, roared into the village in jeeps, looting, shooting, taking whatever they wanted at the point of a gun. What they wanted most was drink and women. The village and its inhabitants were the spoils of war. No one was in command here. The only authority was a rifle, the only argument a bullet in the head or gut.

Dietrich had gone with his grandparents into the village in the morning. By afternoon they had not returned. I was about to go and search for them when Liese's mother appeared, her face ashen, her eyes wild.

'He's dead,' she said. 'They've killed him.'

'Dietrich?'

'No. My husband.'

'Where's Dietrich?'

'In the field, standing near his grandfather.'

I went to the field near the village by a shortcut along the path used by farmers. At first I could not see him, but as I drew nearer I saw that he was kneeling near the body shaking it. '*Grossvater! Grossvater!* Get up. Please, get up,' he cried.

The old man had been shot through the heart and stomach. Dietrich was trembling, ice cold and very pale. I carried him home and put him to bed. He muttered incoherently and fought to keep his eyes open until he fell into an exhausted sleep. The three of them, Liese's mother said, were walking back from the village through the fields when a bunch of Russian soldiers came behind them on a tractor driven at full speed. The men were joyriding and the man at the wheel seemed to have drunk more than the others because the machine was careering about. Liese's parents stopped, afraid they might be run over. Suddenly the tractor spluttered, choked and died. The soldiers couldn't start it up again. They called to the old man and waved their arms about angrily as he moved nearer. They kept shouting at him. He could not understand what they were saying and shook his head. There was more shouting and they began waving their rifles in the air. He realized they wanted diesel and shook his head angrily to tell them he did not have any. One of them shot him dead. Then they left the tractor and made their way back into the village.

The day after we buried Liese's father, her mother was found floating in the river. I thought at first she might have committed suicide (several old people in the village hanged themselves when the war ended) but the doctor said she died of a heart attack and must have lost her footing. Liese took her mother's death harder than her father's. '*We* killed them. If we'd stayed in Waldburg they'd be alive now.' There was no way in which I could make her see the illogicality of her belief. And she blamed me for originating the move from Waldburg. I have observed this so often with Liese: shutters come down in her mind on certain subjects; opinions for which there is no basis become hardened into dogma – permanent, unshakable, hopelessly irrational, so that any sympathy for her becomes drowned in exasperation.

I was in the room upstairs with Liese and the children when a group of Russian soldiers burst in downstairs. I bolted the door, armed myself with my hammer from the toolbox and waited behind the door, asking the children to be silent. We heard shouts and two shots, followed by rapid firing and the sound of smashing glass. After that, silence. Another burst of firing. Silence. Then the sound of a jeep roaring away.

We went downstairs to find that the farmer's wife and daughters were safe; they had locked themselves in on the floor below us. On the ground floor the farmer was bent over in pain, the room around him a shambles. He had been knocked down, he said, with the butt of a rifle.

'They came charging in shouting for drinks. I said I didn't have any, so one of them knocked me down while another fired shots above my head at the painting on the wall. They left me there, went to the kitchen. They ransacked the cupboards. When they found nothing there they sprayed the kitchen with bullets, shattering all the crockery. They came back here, turned their rifles on the walls and shot everything to pieces: family portraits, holy pictures, lamps, glass ornaments, anything in sight. *Himmelkreuz in Donnerwetter!* How am I going to repair the damage?'

I couldn't understand why he had not given them the drink they wanted when he had a well-stocked cellar.

'I'm not going to waste good wine on the likes of them,' he said. 'I paid good money for it.'

Yet a few days later he had to do exactly that. He, his daughters and I were coming in from the fields late in the evening when three soldiers drove into the yard in a cloud of dust.

'My God! The girls!' the farmer said.

The Russians had seen them and were calling out to them.

'Are these the ones who shot up your room?'

'No.'

'Give me the keys to the cellar and welcome them like long-lost brothers.'

I raised my hand in the Communist salute and greeted them with the smattering of Russian picked up from the prisoners I had guarded.

'Have you gone off your rocker?' the farmer said. 'They look as if they've had a skinful already.'

'If you want to save your daughters, do as I say. *Smile!*'

The farmer gave a slight twitch to his mouth.

'Goddammit! *Smile!* Split your face doing it and greet them as comrades.'

He fixed his mouth into a nauseating smile, raised his hand in greeting and invited them into the house. The soldiers looked confused; they could not have been more than eighteen or nineteen. I led them to the most comfortable seats and asked the farmer's daughters to sit next to them. With gesturing and halting Russian, I told them that we too were staunch Communists and wanted to celebrate the arrival of the Russian liberators.

I brought up several bottles from the cellar and we began a bout of drinking that went on until the bottles were empty. I fetched more and still more. We were all comrades together. I sang a German drinking song and asked them to sing. The evening wore on and their songs became sad, tearful ballads of homelands far away. With their permission I placed their rifles in a corner of the room so that they could be more comfortable and stretch their legs. In one of my trips to the cellar I carried the rifles down with me, removed the bullets, and replaced them in the corner. Eventually they could not even sing; they were slumped on the settee.

'We can move them now,' I said.

'Kill them,' the farmer said.

'I don't want to spend the night burying corpses. They'll be missed at barracks and we'll have the Russian army down on the village in reprisal. Help me carry them out.'

I handed each his rifle and, supporting one man at a time between us, the farmer and I piled them into the jeep. I drove them to the other side of the village, three kilometres past the last house and left them there.

When I returned the farmer was grumbling about the amount of drink consumed. 'You didn't have to give them the best wine,' he said. 'I was keeping it for a special occasion.'

'I grabbed whatever was nearest. And besides, this was one.'

23

Dietrich was ill with a fever. In his sleep he called out in delirium. When Liese went to comfort him, he did not recognize her but sat on the bed, eyes wide open, calling out, 'No, no, don't. I can't . . . *Grossvater!*' When she spoke to him, he put his finger to his lips and said, 'Sh! They will hear you. They're coming,' and began to pant and gasp as if he were running. He ate nothing and grew weaker every day.

Martha and the children arrived; she was more agitated than I had ever seen her. Whatever her circumstances, she had always managed to keep herself and the children clean and tidy. Today her dress was crumpled, her hair unbrushed, her face unwashed; the children looked frightened and unusually subdued.

'You asked me to come if I needed help,' she said. 'You can send me away if you like. We'll hide in the woods. But the soldiers are everywhere. We're not going back to the school hall. Never.'

She said that she and the children were in the washroom when they heard shouts and screams and children crying. She thought they were being massacred. She stayed where she was for a very long time. When she felt it was safe to come out again she found that the soldiers had raped all the women. The Bürgermeister had handed them over to the Russians because they threatened that, if he did not, they would rape his wife and daughters. Three children were shot for trying to intervene. Martha hid her face in her hands while her children stood awkwardly, shifting from one foot to another.

'You must stay with us. I'll have a word with the farmer.'

'The widow Roth escaped. She left the school hall the morning after we were admitted – it wasn't good enough for her. She lives with an old couple in their house. I don't know how she persuaded them to take her in.'

The widow Roth came over to our place when I was out working in the fields. What happened then I learned from Martha when she came shouting for me. The widow simpered and smiled and said she had come to repay Liese's kindness in bringing her here. The old couple she lived with had clothes their grandchildren had outgrown.

'You were the first person I thought of, Liese,' she said. 'You can use them for your children. They're giving them away. Come with me now and you can choose the best.'

'Why can't you bring them here?' Martha asked.

'Oh, I couldn't do that. The old lady is most particular who she gives the clothes to. She insists on seeing you before handing them over.'

'I can't leave Dietrich. He's ill. I'll come when he's better.'

'They may have gone by then.' She bustled over to peer at Dietrich. 'He won't mend if he doesn't eat. I have medicine that will stimulate his appetite. Would you like it for your little boy?'

'Rest is the best medicine for children,' Martha said. 'Pumping them full of drugs can only do harm.'

'It's not a drug – it's a herbal remedy. It's quite harmless. I've taken it often and it never fails. Come with me now. He's asleep. You can get the medicine and the clothes and be back in no time. He won't even know you've gone.'

'Will you stay with Dietrich?' Liese asked Martha. 'I'll be very quick.'

'The streets are not safe.'

'They were quite safe when I came here,' the widow said. 'I wouldn't suggest it otherwise. There wasn't a soul around. The house is quite nearby.'

Liese went with her. As soon as they stepped inside the widow's house they were surrounded by half a dozen soldiers. One of them took the widow, kicking and screaming, into another room. 'You promised, you promised you wouldn't touch me if I brought her to you,' she shouted. The rest of them took Liese upstairs and raped her.

She stumbled back to the farmhouse and collapsed in Martha's arms. Martha got the story from her in bits and pieces. She prepared a tub of hot water for her and bathed her. Only then did she come outside shouting for me to come in at once.

Liese sat in a corner, her hair lank and wet, a figure turned to stone. Her head was bent and when she raised it there were bruises on her face. But it was the look she gave me that was shocking: it was the look of a dumb animal that cannot understand the pain it endures, haunted, harrowed, howling in silent anguish.

'Why didn't you tell me? I could have gone instead of you,' I said.

'She went for the child,' Martha said, 'she went for the medicine. Only there *was* no medicine. It was a trap. That treacherous bitch! I'm glad they killed her.'

So was I. Had she been alive, I'd have killed her myself.

When at last Liese spoke she said, 'Oh God, I wish I were dead.'

'It will pass,' I said rather stupidly, for want of anything else to say.

'No, it won't. I feel . . . I feel dirty . . . filthy, like a stinking pond covered with slime . . . and the reek of it will be with me always.'

As I looked at Liese then, her face blotched and ugly, her eyes tormented, her body more like a shapeless sack than ever, I, who had wandered so far away from her, felt my heart breaking with pity and stirring with something akin to the faint shadow of love, for I saw near her the ghost of that slender, golden girl with wide, wondering eyes in that enchanted summer long, long ago.

Martha took on all the household tasks. She nursed Dietrich back to health, looked after all the children, cooked the meals, washed, mended and ironed our clothes. She glowed with effort. She kept the children out of Liese's way and removed herself from the room when I came in, recalling some imaginary domestic task that demanded immediate attention. When I told her what a help she was to us all, she shrugged her shoulders in pleased embarrassment.

'I like to help,' she said. 'I do what I can. I'm not clever or beautiful, but I know how to keep a house clean and I like to pay my way. I've been doing it all my life.'

That blunt, graceless speech was the closest she ever came to receiving thanks. She was, I thought, remarkably like our drays – strong, dogged, utterly reliable.

24

The Bürgermeister came to the farm, he said, to pay a courtesy visit. This was the man who had turned over a hall full of refugee women to Russian soldiers, and yet he looked perfectly normal. Dressed formally in a grey business suit, he was a small, square man with a ruddy complexion, a dome of a head that was bald, wearing round, steel-rimmed glasses and with a brisk, official manner.

'Just passing. Thought I'd drop by and see how you were all settling in. I take it you are all well? And comfortable? Good, good. Do you need anything? Difficult times, as we all know, but if I can help at all, that's what I'm here for.'

He smiled a great deal as if he were at an official reception and yet an occasional glance flashed a predatory anxiety. The bland words came a little too glibly, as if they had been carefully rehearsed.

I assumed the blank expression of a country yokel and made my speech slow-witted. Whatever game he was up to, two could play at it. The farmer was surprised but shrewd enough to say nothing. Eventually after more official noises about concern for our welfare, the Bürgermeister got to the point.

'I wonder if you could do me a favour. I'm not one to forget my friends. I have a friend who owns a farm some distance away – he's fallen ill and there's no one around to help. If his crops are not taken in he will be ruined. Several people from the village have already volunteered to help but the farm is large and more hands are needed. Could you oblige me, do you think? It would be temporary, only a couple of weeks.

You'll be paid, have board and lodging provided, and transport as well.'

'I've my hands full here,' the farmer grumbled. 'I can't spare anyone at the moment.'

'Of course. Quite. I understand fully. But when the pressure of work eases off here, as it undoubtedly will, you'll be able to spare this man and some of the women also, perhaps, to help someone out of trouble? In these difficult times, if Germans don't help each other, who will?'

'Oh, yezzir,' I said, making my face as oaf-like as possible, 'I'll certainly help ye when work here's done.'

'Good, good. I'll look in again in a week or so.'

The farmer was about to protest but I intervened. 'I'll look for'rard to it. Thank ye, zir, thank ye,' my face assuming a mask of gratitude, gullibility and deference. 'It were kind of ye to come, zir.'

'What are you playing at?' the farmer said, as soon as the Bürgermeister left.

'I'm playing for time. I want him off our backs for a while, long enough to make inquiries from the families he's named as volunteers and find out what conditions are like on the farm. I smell a rat.'

We discovered that the Bürgermeister had indeed visited all the families he had mentioned; he had visited every single house in the village and told the same tale. Several volunteers had already left; none had returned. The farm was at Hagibor. I know nothing of the place at the time but I was still very suspicious of the Bürgermeister's story. I smelt danger in much the same way as one can sense on a battlefield, even when conditions seem wholly quiet, that an attack is on the way. There was talk in the village that a Czech civilian government was being set up in Prague and an edict was expected any day ordering all Germans to return to their place of origin. I decided to clear out.

We left Erzbach, taking Martha and the children with us, to return to Waldburg. It was only much later, when I met a man from Hagibor that I learned there was no farm there. Hagibor was a concentration camp set up by the Czechs, where German civilians were used for slave labour and punishment. The men were beaten to death, the women given over to Russian soldiers every night. In the early days unsuspecting volunteers went there, sent by patriots like the Bürgermeister; later on the prisoners were brought in by Czech 'partisans'.

25

Now, as I begin yet again to set down that part of my story that is my vision of hell, my flesh begins to crawl. I have forced myself to record these things so many times, and each time I have abandoned the task soon after it was begun. I, who was accustomed to seeing horrific injuries in the war, find myself nauseated at the prospect before me. The attempt to put down on paper what was experienced in that single year after the war, when we who were young grew old, is like being stretched out on an operating table and disembowelled without an anaesthetic.

The atrocities performed under Hitler's National Socialist Party are well known and the perpetrators (at least, those who were caught) condemned at the Nuremberg trials. But after the war ended what was done in Czechoslovakia and Poland to German civilians is unknown and unnoticed. For the perpetrators it was something-that-would-never-be-known; for the world at large it is something-that-never-happened because it-could-never-happen: such orgies of brutality that it would require a diseased, deranged imagination to invent them. Human nature is not so different after all. These men, the monsters of history, existed in Germany under Hitler, in Czechoslovakia under Beneš. They exist now in Britain, in America, in Russia, in every country in the world; all it needs is a crisis to reveal their inherent bestiality. The fabulous beasts of legend are with us, always.

All through the war years there was virtually no resistance by Czechs to the German occupation forces. To whip up anti-German feeling, the British Secret Service trained a group of Czechs in exile and parachuted them into Czechoslovakia to assassinate the SS Commander Heydrich. The mission was a success. Heydrich was killed and the savage SS reprisal for his death created the climate the British had calculated it would produce. The first act of 'resistance' by the Czechs was in April, just before the war ended, when the Czechs fell on the civilian population in Prague and butchered them. Their leaders, Beneš and Masaryk, spent the war years safely in exile. On 13 May, when President Beneš returned to Prague, his arrival was celebrated by setting alight lines of Germans as human torches. Revolutionary guards broadcast the message from Prague: 'Death to all Germans. Kill the Germans wherever you meet them. Women, children, Germans of all ages – every German is our mortal enemy. Now is the chance to exterminate our enemies. Let us make an end of them.'

On arrival in Waldburg we drove straight to Max's bakery. His father seemed to have shrunk into himself; his bright blue eyes were dulled and sunken, his head quite bald now, his generous, wide mouth, which resembled Max's so closely, turned down at the corners. His wife was dead, his daughters raped and killed in his house, their heads battered against the kitchen table in the struggle. There was no news of Max.

'You can move into my house,' he said. 'I could do with another pair of hands at the bakery.'

His house was next to the bakery, a solid, stone-built, square building on three floors with walls two metres thick. Rounded arches and pillars gave its façade an air of quiet distinction. The stone was a pale grey which turned silver in the sun. Double sets of windows at the outer and inner sides of the walls made it warm in winter, cool in summer; brightly painted green shutters made it a house that seemed to smile.

I told him that I had Martha and her children with me.

'They'll have to stay here with you. They can have my daughters' room. Her house has been taken by a Czech and there's no way she'll get it back. If she tries she'll be sent to a camp. They'll be safe in my house. The ground floor's been taken over by a Russian officer and his staff.'

I looked at him sceptically.

'No, really, they're allright. Decent fellows. They behave very correctly. They've never threatened or harmed me, and the major's batman is very helpful. When their own soldiers tried to burst into the house he chased them away. They're our insurance against their own people and the Czechs.'

'I've two women and two girls with me. You want me to put them in the same house? After what they did to your daughters?'

'That was before they arrived. If they'd been here, my daughters would be alive. These are good men. Time and again it's Russian officers who've saved Germans from the Czechs. The day the major arrived in Waldburg the Czechs had brought in a lorryload of thugs – convicts, they looked like – armed with staves and brickbats. You know the bridge that workers from the brick factory use to cross the river? These thugs were waiting for them there as they were on their way home. All other exits from the factory were barred and they were set upon as they reached the bridge. They threw them into the river, everyone, men, women, children, even some women near the river bank who were wheeling babies in prams – all of them, babies, prams and all, flung into the river, beaten and held down by staves until they drowned. It was only when the major arrived that the thugs were dispersed. God knows how many more would've drowned otherwise.'

During my time in that house I did not have much to do with the Russians. The major's batman conversed in broken German with Max's father. He and I greeted each other whenever our paths crossed, but I never stopped long enough to talk to him at length. I liked what I saw of him: a round, freckled face, close-cropped brown hair, a trim figure neatly turned out, a man with an air of quiet competence who seemed to observe nothing but saw a great deal. He often stopped to talk to Martha; Liese avoided him. 'Don't worry,' he'd say. 'You are safe here, I promise.' Martha referred to him as 'the don't worry man'.

Our room was at the top of the house, comfortably furnished with beds, a wardrobe and a chest of drawers; windows on two sides looked out onto the road in front, the river and open country at the back. One wall, which seemed to be part of the roof, sloped down diagonally from floor to ceiling, with wooden beams and rafters. In spite of the batman's reassurances I felt the women and girls needed a hiding place. I examined the house from outside and saw that the garage was an integral part of the house, situated on the same side as our room. The roof sloped down above the garage and yet, judging from its size, it seemed that our room stopped short at the point where the garage began. This meant that on the other side of the sloping wall of our room was a space measuring the length and width of the garage. Somehow, if I could get access to that space, it would make a good hiding place.

I discussed the matter with Max's father. 'If I could make a trapdoor into that space, it'd be ideal. It's impossible to detect from the outside.'

'But how are you going to conceal it inside the room? You'll have to cut through the timbers.'

'It's possible,' I took him upstairs. 'You see the horizontal timbers covered by these vertical planks for strengthening? If I make the trapdoor by cutting *behind* the vertical planks and hinge it so that it opens inwards, there'll be no evidence of a door there at all. It will look exactly as it does now: part of the house roof.'

'It'll mean a lot of work. We really are quite safe, you know.'

'For how long? What happens when the batman is asleep or away on an errand?'

'Very well, but be careful. I don't want the roof damaged.'

I worked on the trap door every evening when I came home from the bakery, deadening the sound by closing the windows and stuffing paper and sacking against the door. One of the older children was posted as a lookout on the stairs. When I had sawn each plank, Martha carefully swept up the sawdust and put it in the stove. At last the trapdoor was finished. Liese and Martha scoured the hiding place and covered the floor with sacking. Every evening Liese and Martha, Erika, who was ten, and Maria, who was eleven, slept in there.

In the days that followed more and more Czechs moved into Waldburg and the surrounding areas. A number of decrees were issued by President Beneš and the Národni Výbor, the Czech National Council, defining the position of Germans in Czechoslovakia:

All Germans are to wear a white armband with a black 'N' for *Němec* (the Czech word for 'German').

No German is allowed to use public transport.

All Germans are forbidden to walk on the pavement.

All Germans must surrender gold, silver, jewellery, radios, cameras and any other valuable items, under pain of death, to the Czech authorities.

All Germans will be issued with special ration cards (on which there was no provision for meat, eggs, milk, cheese or fruit).

All Germans may only use the shops and streets during certain permitted hours.

All Germans aged thirteen and over must report, under pain of death, to the labour exchange, which will assign them to suitable work.

All Germans under thirteen are forbidden any form of education.

Concentration camps are being set up for the punishment of criminals, members of the Nazi Party, collaborators, unreliable elements and enemies of the people.

The last decress cast so wide a net that it could include just about anyone. *Koncentračni tábor*, the concentration camps, had their names changed later to *internačni tábor*, internment camps, and *shromážd ovaci středisko*, collection camps, on the principle that if you call a dung heap a rose it will begin to smell sweet.

Every Czech returning to Waldburg claimed to be a partisan. If a 'partisan' wanted a German's house or shop or farm or factory, he simply took it – by turning the owner and his family out onto the street if he was tender-hearted, or into a concentration camp if he was not. In our area eventually, apart from private houses, the brick factory, the brewery, the power plant, and, farther afield, the coalmines, were taken over by Czechs, in addition to all the farms in the region. They were, after all, only doing what Beneš maintained, that it was better to let thistles grow in German fields than allow Germans to cultivate them.

As long as we remained indoors the Russian major and his batman were our safeguard. But out on the streets the butchering began. Because I could understand Czech (and speak it tolerably) from my national service days, I thought it less dangerous to move out of doors without my armband. I saw a group of Czechs pounce on three Germans who, they claimed, were members of the Nazi Party. They tied them to a tree, poured petrol over them and set them alight. I saw a young man wearing the uniform of the Waffen SS, the fighting arm of the service, dragged in front of a group of German women who were forced to watch him being blinded.

Schmidt's old ironmongery store was destroyed by a grenade explosion one morning, killing everyone in it. I was outside the shop and had seen two Czech youths larking about outside, throwing a hand grenade to each other. I saw them enter the shop and the explosion followed a few minutes later. A group of partisans arrived to see the Russian major, demanding a hundred German civilians to be shot in reprisal because, they said, the Germans had booby-trapped the shop. The major refused. The partisans reduced their demand to fifty. The major still refused. The partisans went away, rounded up twenty German men and women off the streets and shot them – first in the genitals, then in the stomach, then in the head. As the dying lay screaming, the partisan leader said, 'German blood is pig's urine. What are you complaining about?'

26

Max came home. He had been very ill in hospital in Berlin. Looking at him now it was difficult to recognize my friend. I remembered him as a roly-poly figure with a round, good-natured face, mischievous eyes and an effervescent, exuberant personality. The man who returned was a stranger: pale, sickly, with a grey pallor and sunken eyes, his body shrivelled to a frail shadow. Only the mouth, wide and generous, and the broad hands with stubby fingers were the same. He was sullen, brooding, embittered, fuelled by rage.

He refused to say anything about his journey. When his father persisted, rather unwisely, in pressing him with questions, he screamed at him, 'Shut up! Leave me alone. I don't want to talk about it. Can't you understand? I don't want to talk about it.' It was only with the children that he seemed to find a semblance of his former self. Little Dietrich, especially, became very attached to him. Max whittled toys out of wood for him and, much later, began the grand project of a pair of skis for Christmas.

Liese realized that she was pregnant. I had seen her in dark moods before but never like this. She was like a woman possessed, beating her forehead with her fists, weeping, shouting, spitting abuse. 'God in heaven, isn't it enough, what they've done already? Why should I be torn apart by a bastard who'll have his father's face? Which face? Which out of all those with their burning eyes and groping hands?'

'The baby might be a girl, might look like you,' I said.

'It's not a baby. It's a monster brought into being by a

monstrous act. You're a man. You can never understand what it means to carry a child for months on end, watching your body become grotesque in the process. It's only bearable because of love. Without it, it's a disease.'

Nothing I said could comfort her. Whatever I said was wrong, inadequate, hopeless. So wild and reckless was her behaviour that I began to think she might do something desperate. It was Martha who prevented this. She went to the church and brought Father Klein back with her. He seemed largely unchanged. The long, intelligent face had its lines of weariness deepened and a few new ones etched on his forehead, the fine hair was thinning at the top but lay in a neat circle hugging the head as always, the bright blue eyes were alert and kindly as ever. He sat alone with Liese for over an hour. I don't know what he said to her or she to him but afterwards the wildness and desperation left her. Gradually she became her normal, abrasive self again.

The Russian major and his staff were moving out to another town. The batman would not leave without saying goodbye to each of us. Max's father thanked him for protecting us.

He shrugged his shoulders. 'I couldn't allow an officer's quarters to be overrun by rabble. Some of our men, I'm afraid, are no better than animals. But compared to the Czechs they're angels. Be careful now.' He turned to me. 'How old is your son and the other boy?'

'Leo's eleven, Franz is twelve.'

'The Czechs are sending boys of thirteen to the coalmines. They don't last long there. When these two turn thirteen keep them well hidden.' He looked me full in the face and said quietly, 'I don't think they'll be able to find them upstairs.'

I thought that I had built the hiding place so secretly that no one except ourselves knew of it.

He saw the surprise in my face. 'I have a wife and children as well. Look,' he said, pulling out his wallet and extracting a photograph curled at the corners. A pretty, buxom young woman smiled out of the picture, three children standing near her. 'Tanya,

Natasha, Yuri, Ditya,' he said. Handling the photograph as if it were a precious jewel, he returned it to his wallet.

'How long before you see them again?'

He shrugged and made a grimace. 'Too long.'

'Have you heard anything of Potsdam? There are rumours that we'll all be thrown out.'

'I only know the big brass are meeting there. There's talk of resettling Germans from Hungary, Poland and Czechoslovakia.'

'But only recently Mr Churchill broadcast on the BBC about protecting the rights of minorities. *We*'re a minority.'

'You heard the broadcast?'

'I heard *of* it,' Max's father said quickly. 'This has been our homeland for centuries – since 1284, and church records of that time say we've been here "past the memory of man". Where can three and a half million people go for resettlement?'

'I hope it won't come to that. I must go now. *Auf wiedersehen.* And take care.'

The next day a Czech took over the house and bakery, moving not only into the ground floor which the Russians had occupied but also the floor above, so that Max and his father, with Martha and her children, had to move into our room at the top. Since the Czech knew nothing about the business, he allowed Max, his father and me to work in the bakery as unpaid servants.

Max was raging.

'Be quiet and listen!' his father said. 'As long as we're his servants the Czechs can't press-gang us for hard labour elsewhere. He's let us remain in the house. He could have thrown us out on the street or in a camp. We've been lucky.'

'Oh yes, we've been very lucky,' Max said. 'We're being allowed to live in one room in our own house and work as his servants in our own bakery. What more can we want?'

'One of these days you'll get us all killed. You'll not be satisfied till then.'

I looked at Max's angry, embittered face and knew there was no reasoning with him.

*

I had been sent on an errand to one of the shops in the High Street and had just stepped outside when there was a sudden commotion. A group of lorries arrived. A gang of Czechs emerged from one of them and unloaded sacks of broken glass which they strewed thickly all along the narrow road. Two groups of Czechs sealed off the road at each end. From the other lorries about forty or fifty German prisoner-of-war, some of them boys who could not have been more than sixteen, were herded out. They were ordered to take off their trousers and forced to crawl on bare hands and knees from one end of the High Street to the other, while the Czechs, who had ranged themselves on either side of the road, urged them on with blows from clubs, rifle butts, staves and iron bars.

I wanted to rush out and stop them, I wanted to cry out, 'Don't do it. Oh, don't!' I wanted to help, I wanted to do so many things, something, anything, to prevent what was happening. But I could do nothing. I stood rooted to the spot in disbelief, my eyes streaming with tears (I, who am not given to weeping), and was not aware that I was crying. I saw them crunching along. Several fell on their faces and, rather than resume their journey, abandoned themselves to being clubbed to death. Others crawled on and on, their shredded limbs as indistinguishable pulp beneath them. The air grew thick with blood and screams of the dying. One of them, endurance almost spent, crouched gasping for breath, and as he saw a Czech swing his iron bar towards him, raised his arm to ward off the blow. I saw his upturned face just before he was smashed down. It was Friedrich. His eyes were glazed as he looked at the man who beat him to death. Years later I saw the same face, a figure in just such an attitude with one arm raised, looking at his tormentor, in a small village church in Germany, in one of the stations of the cross. The sculptor had captured that very scene, with Christ given Friedrich's face, carrying his cross urged on with whips and staves by guards in Roman uniform but with the unmistakable faces of Czechs.

When at last every prisoner had been killed, the Czechs ordered several Germans – myself included among them – to clear up the mess of corpses and broken glass. We dug a mass grave, filled it with bodies, went back and swept the street clean until nothing, save the blood that had soaked into the earth, remained.

I could not tell Martha that Friedrich was involved in what I had seen. I told Max instead.

'I'll tell her that you met someone who'd served with him in his regiment, who told you for certain that he was killed at the front.'

Martha received the news stocially, but that night and for many nights afterwards, though she tried to be as quiet as possible, Liese said, she could be heard weeping.

Max became increasingly irritable. Living in a single room with nine others grated on his nerves. He coughed a great deal, long paroxysms that wore him out and left him breathless. For some reason the sight of the women and girls retiring into the hiding place every evening made him furious.

One evening after the trapdoor had been shut on them he said, 'We live like animals in a cage while our keepers lord it in our own house.'

'They don't mind,' I said. 'They're used to it now. When the boys become thirteen they'll have to stay in there all day and all night.'

'They're children. Even animals have freedom to roam the woods. They can't be cooped up for twenty-four hours day after day.'

'They'll have to, if they're to survive.'

'Survive, survive!' Max shouted. 'That's all you can think of. Survive at all costs. These Czechs need to be wiped off the face of the earth. Kill the bloody lot of them.'

'You sound exactly like Heinrich. Here, take this,' I said, handing him my hammer. 'Go ahead. Go out and kill as many Czechs as you can. It's as quick a way as any of committing suicide.'

He glared at me and threw the hammer at my head. I saw it coming and ducked. Max hurled himself upon me and screamed abuse. He did not have my reach or size, or, in his present condition, the strength to injure me. I held him off easily until the fury of his blows subsided. He sank into a chair, a crumpled, helpless figure, sucking in his breath in great gasps.

'I'm sorry, Martin. It's not you I hate.'

'You've changed so much. I've done everything I could think of to bring back the man you used to be.'

'The man I used to be died long ago. He died many times, and I watched him. I thought it would stop hurting after a while, but it doesn't.'

'I wish I knew how to help you.'

'You can't. No one can.' He looked into the distance and said, 'It's not dying that takes courage. It's living.'

27

One morning a group of partisans came into the bakery.

'Which one is it?' said a thick-set, square-jawed man who seemed to be their leader.

'That one,' said a short, dumpy Czech who was with them. 'That's him, Captain.' He was pointing at me. There was something vaguely familiar about him.

'You're sure?'

'Certain. He was in the Freikorps.'

'There's some mistake,' I said. 'I've never been in the Freikorps. In fact . . .'

Before I could finish the captain shouted me down. 'Lies won't save you now.'

Max and his father protested on my behalf but the captain silenced them by threatening them with his rifle.

'Where have you hidden your weapons?'

'I've never had any weapons. I was never in the Freikorps. I . . .'

I was interrupted by a blow in the stomach. As I doubled up, two more blows on my back brought me down on the floor. 'Don't speak unless you're told to.'

I was led away to one of two lorries waiting outside. As I passed by the man who had pointed at me, a sideways jerk of his head, a trick of light from the doorway which now illuminated his face, slotted him back in my memory. It was Wazlawik, the Czech customs official I'd saved from Katzer and his gang. Grovelling, treacherous creep! He seemed to be ingratiating himself with the captain at my expense.

*

Koncentrační Tábor – Concentration Camp – the sign over the gates announced. Of the fifty-one concentration camps in Czechoslovakia, several were known as death camps. I, with forty-nine other Germans that day, arrived at one of the death camps, Thomasdorf. It was much smaller than the vast complexes of Theresienstadt or Maltheuern but just as efficient in carrying out its programme. The camp had housed a hundred Russian prisoners-of-war during the war; it now contained two hundred German men and boys, several as old as seventy or as young as thirteen. At the perimeter there was a double barbed-wire fence, within which was the main building, a large long hut divided into sections. The other buildings consisted of the guardhouse, with the punishment cells next to it, a kitchen and dining hut, the *marotka*, the medical hut, and a small hut used as a barber's shop. There was a hut for washing clothes, but the prisoners washed themselves in the stream that ran through the camp.

On arrival we were made to line up in the yard and place everything we owned in front of us: watches, tobacco, wedding rings, matches, all personal possessions, which were confiscated by the guards. We were told to stand with our arms above our heads. The commandant came to look at us – a powerfully built man who was a Czech but wore Russian uniform during the day and SS uniform in the evening. The guards too, who were all Czechs, wore a variety of uniforms, some Russian, some Nazi, while those with any special authority wore the SS uniform. All had a red enamel star on their shirts and a red badge on their caps. It was like a fancy-dress party where no one had quite got the costume right.

'How many?' the commandant asked one of the guards.

'Fifty.'

The commandant started counting from one end of the line. His method was to stand in front of each prisoner and hit him with a cosh on the forehead. Those who fell were kicked viciously and told to get up. Several old men could not do so. More kicks from the guards, and when they still did not get up, they were dragged away and shot for 'disobeying orders'. When my turn came I tried to ride the blow. Even so, I staggered, but I managed to stay upright.

When the commandant had finished counting he said, 'German blood is pigshit. No one who has entered this camp today will leave it alive. Every one of you will have to be punished for the crimes committed by Germans.'

Photographs, souvenirs, personal papers, letters, which had now been sifted from the valuables taken from the prisoners, were brought before him, placed in a heap and ceremoniously burned.

We were kept standing there, our arms above our heads, for several hours. Every time anyone dropped his arms (and it was impossible not to do so) he was beaten by the guards, who carried an armoury of weapons: sticks, iron bars, clubs and whips of various length.

Eventually we were allowed to go to the barber's shop, where our heads were close-shaven, and then taken for individual interviews with the commandant. I was accompanied by three guards. The commandant was at his desk on which a row of gleaming knives was arranged. He stretched his huge arms, picked up one of the knives and threw it at me. It whistled past my shoulder and thudded in the wall. One after the other they came. I watched his eyes under the heavy, bushy black eyebrows and stood quite still, feeling I was more likely to be hit if I moved. Was he perhaps a former circus artiste robbed of his chance of fame by the war, working out his frustrations in an exhibition of skill that drew terror as applause from his captive audience? When I was encircled with knives he ordered one of the guards to return them to the desk. One was slightly out of alignment; he pushed it back with the tip of his finger. Then just as casually he gave a signal to a guard, who delivered a punch in my stomach.

'Say *Děkuji*, I thank you, to the commandant.

'*Děkuji.*' And then the interrogation began, the commandant asking the questions, the guards performing a ritual.

'Were you in the Freikorps? Were you in the SS? Were you in the SA?'

Although these were phrased as questions they were delivered as statements, for every answer received blows and after each blow '*Děkuji*' was expected. I fell down and was kicked in the head, the back, the ribs, the balls. One guard pulled and twisted my arm as if trying to dislocate it. Later I saw several prisoners with arms wrenched out of their sockets. I managed to get up and was smashed down again. I was turned over on my stomach and beaten all over with sticks. '*Děkuji! Děkuji! Děkuji!*' until I was dragged out and flung into one of the punishment cells behind the guardroom.

I did not know how long I lay on the concrete floor in that small, bare cell. I couldn't move. My clothes were stuck to me, clotted with blood. I was left there, I did not care for how long provided I was left alone, without food or water. Had these been available, I could not have eaten or drunk anything, since my lips were swollen so badly that they were glued together.

I learned later that I was left there for two days and nights. On the third day a guard came and shouted to me to get up and report for work. I tried to but could not. The guard went away. Some time later a prisoner came and said that if I did not report for work I would be shot. He helped me up and took me to the work-duty hut where I was told to report to the *marotka* as a medical orderly. I collected my prison clothes – a coarse shirt with number 96 in front and a large white swastika and KT on the back.

I hobbled and lurched into the *marotka*. 'I'm reporting for work duty as a medical orderly,' I said. Looking back on it now, it seems grotesquely funny, but it was no laughing matter at the time.

There were three other medical orderlies there with a doctor in charge, all of them prisoners. The 'doctor' was a masseur from a sanatorium.

'There's no doctor here,' he said, 'and no medical supplies except bandages and cold water. An army surgeon comes round once in a while but only to rubber-stamp prisoners' death certificates. Sit here and let me see if I can clean you up. Reception committee?'

I gave a very slight nod for it was extremely painful to move my head. I was very thirsty and indicated this. He fed me water from a spoon, dribbling it in at one corner of my balloon mouth. As he worked with cold compresses he said, 'It's always the same. He kills several on the day of arrival; the unfortunate ones die later. You'll live, I think.'

I'll live, I thought, if only to be revenged on Wazlawik. I should have let Katzer finish him off as he'd intended. Good deeds have a way of catching up with me in the most extraordinary manner. 'One of my few Christian acts,' Liese called the saving of Wazlawik, and its outcome has been worse than anything that resulted from my numerous vices, which nearly always brought pleasure. It is a bizarre situation. I was kicked out of the German army because of my Jewish origins. If they had found proof of my Jewishness I would have been sent to a German concentration camp and crisped to a cinder. The end of the war, which set free remaining Jews from camps, has put me in one – on the word of a man whose life I'd saved.

Albert Fischer, the masseur, had been here for nearly three months, sent here when the sanatorium he worked in was taken over by a Czech. He was a quiet, middle-aged man with patient brown eyes and gentle hands.

'I was accused of not turning over my valuables to the state. They searched and looted my house but found nothing. It made no difference. At least some of us know what we're accused of, even if the charges are trumped up. Half the poor devils in this camp have no idea why they're here at all; many were rounded up off the street. It's one way of providing a constant supply of slave labour, but I don't know why they bring in boys of thirteen and fourteen – they don't last long.'

He began unrolling the bandages. 'Did they learn about camps from Hitler, I wonder, and he in turn learn about them from the British who invented them in the Boer War? There was a Jew here from Auschwitz. He'd spent three years there, came out, and the Czechs arrested him on the street. He was treated like a monkey here: dressed in a red cap and red jacket, and made to push a wheelbarrow, do tricks for the commandant, like jumping about and running faster and faster with his barrow. "Hitler didn't do his job properly with the Jews," the commandant said, "he should have finished them off." One guard rode in the barrow, another jumped on the Jew's shoulders to make him run faster – ran him into the ground and killed him.'

He told me of the camp routine: up at 5 a.m., roll call and early-morning exercises out of doors, breakfast, work details, lunch at twelve. Back to work till seven, roll call and punishments out of doors, supper, and bed at nine.

'I'll cover you for today,' he said, 'but from tomorrow, even if you think you're dying and have to crawl outside, see that you turn up for morning roll call and exercises. Otherwise you'll be a marked man. You're lucky to be sent to the *marotka*. Most of the men work on road gangs hacking a new road through the forest. The lucky few are collected for work outside the camp.'

He showed me to an inner room which had a mattress filled with wood shavings on the floor. I lay down and slept like someone drugged.

Just before nine that evening Albert shook me awake, fed me some water and helped me to my hut. It was like a railway compartment built of logs and housed fifty men, who slept on two-tiered bunk beds on mattresses filled with wood shavings. At either end were latrine buckets, used at night, emptied in the morning. Prisoners were not allowed in the huts during the day, and when they came in at nine not even the stench that clung to them and seemed ingrained in the wood, prevented them from falling asleep. Now, years later, when I see a picture of a log cabin, the stinking air of the camp huts, the smell of sweat and pus and human excrement assaults the senses and the ghosts of the past come striding through the dark.

28

Next morning I woke to the shouts of guards and the clatter of clubs run to and fro across the log walls of the hut. After several attempts I managed to get up and fall in line for roll call. We were made to do physical jerks whose purpose can only have been to provide amusement for the commandant and his deputy. Any prisoner who did not stand in a straight line was beaten. All commands were given in Czech; several prisoners who did not understand the language and were not quick enough to imitate the rest were beaten. Three men whose shoes were not cleaned properly were each given fifteen blows with a stick.

At last we were dismissed for breakfast. This consisted of a mug of black liquid called 'coffee' and the day's ration of 250 grammes of bread made from dirty flour mixed with ground horse chestnuts. I did not know on that first day that it was to last for the evening meal as well; I was so hungry that I ate it all, softening it in the coffee and pushing the mash through my still swollen lips.

Work details lined up. Lorries arrived with Czech employers who came to collect their free labour force. I went to the *marotka*. Albert let me rest in the *marotka* as much as possible, setting me to work only at those times when he knew the guards would look in.

Lunch was the main meal of the day. It was always a vegetable soup, that is hot water with small bits of potato and old, dried-up carrots so tough that even prolonged boiling had not softened them. Supper was a mug of black coffee. This was our diet every day – less than the food at Belsen mentioned in the Nuremberg trials.

Gradually most of my wounds healed: my broken ribs knit together, my lips subsided. I was left with an occasional ringing in my ears and a permanent diagonal scar along my forehead. If I had been as handsome as a film star it would have been most upsetting; having a face like a frog to start with had its compensations.

My work at the *marotka* consisted of attending to the injured, carrying in those who were dying, carrying out the dead to be buried in pits in the forest. We were never short of patients. New entrants replaced the dead at regular intervals. Before I handed over the bodies for burial I searched their pockets for bread and ate it. I learned to keep half my bread ration for the evening and to make it last as long as possible by eating it slowly, rolling it round and round on the tongue. I learned to push my way to the front of the queue at lunchtime because there was a chance of finding some vegetables in the soup.

Sometimes the commandant stood where the soup was handed out. Each prisoner had to say '*Děkuji*' to him. Those who could not pronounce the word correctly had their soup taken away and received a blow from the cosh instead. Old Paul, who was seventy, deaf from blows on his ears and very nervous, shook uncontrollably as he took his bowl and accidentally spilt the soup over the commandant's boots. He was taken away and beaten by guards every day until he died.

The same fetish was made of pronunciation at morning roll call when a sixty-year-old schoolteacher was given fifteen lashes for not saying '*Děkuji*' correctly. He was then asked to say the word again. The commandant was not satisfied, so the punishment was repeated five more times since the man could not pronounce the word to the commandant's standards. We carried him to the *marotka* like a piece of raw meat on a butcher's slab.

Every evening at roll call, and sometimes in the morning, punishments were meted out. These did not follow as cause and effect but were completely arbitrary. Pairs of prisoners were made to stand in front of each other and hit each other on the face. If their blows did not seem sufficiently convincing, the commandant and his deputy showed them by doing the job themselves. Pairs of prisoners were made to suck up dirty water from the ground and spit it in each other's faces. Half a dozen prisoners would be told to keep running round the camp boundary until they fell with exhaustion, when they were beaten by the guards. A group of prisoners would be told to crouch down and hop backwards and forwards across the yard or crawl on their elbows and bellies.

I was convinced at the time that the commandant was insane: his love of fancy dress, his exhibitionism with knives, his open enjoyment of cruelty, all seemed to indicate a sick mind. But now I'm not so sure, for I have heard of other prisoners from other camps who suffered systematic cruelty in much the same way. Theresienstadt, Hagibor, Maltheuern, Jauernig, Adelsdorf . . . the line stretches long.

One evening two brothers aged fifteen and sixteen escaped from their work gang in the woods. The next day they were caught and brought back to the camp. Everyone else escaped punishment at the evening roll call, which was devoted to making an example of them. Swastikas were carved on their bare bottoms; they were then beaten insensible and dragged into the woods where they were shot.

'If a single other prisoner escapes,' said the commandant, 'I shall kill the lot of you and get another two hundred for the camp.'

Of my time at Thomasdorf I remember very few names. We who were there were not companions in misery but each man on his own, impaled upon the sword of his own suffering. There was no time or inclination or capacity to think, outside of one's own skin and bones, of other people. Pain is the most selfish of all sensations and living in it constantly makes a man blind and deaf to anything else. I had stopped thinking about my family too. It wasn't a deliberate act of will, simply that they faded and receded until they were not there any longer. No visits from relatives were allowed. Had they been, the distance they would have had to walk made visits impossible. Writing letters was forbidden. In theory relatives were allowed to bring parcels of food and clothing for prisoners, but very few arrived and these were confiscated by the guards.

29

Among a new batch of prisoners I saw a small, slight figure that looked familiar. With his head shaved and in prison clothes he looked more vulnerable than ever. He was limping. It was Father Klein. Here he was, back in my life again, my shadow that walked everywhere with me. Try as I will, I can never be free of him. He was detailed to one of the outside working parties so I could only speak to him after supper.

'Thank God you're still alive, Martin,' he said. 'Your family's safe and well.'

'Good. And the others? Max and his father? Martha and her children?'

'They're all safe.' His face was badly bruised and one side of it swollen.

'What brought you in here?'

'When I heard you'd been arrested, I went to vouch for you before the People's Council. Do you know who's thick as thieves with them now? Josef Katzer, who's a staunch Communist and claims he's always been one. He's paying off old scores on a number of people and put the finger on me as a collaborator.'

'And they believed his word against yours?'

'It's only temporary. The truth's bound to come out sooner or later.'

'The truth? Truth's irrelevant here. The reception committee showed you that.'

'I got off lighter than most. We're in God's hands.'

'The only God here is the commandant. Can't you see what's happening around you?'

'Yes, and so does He. I trust Him, Martin. He never betrays a trust.'

'Why has he put you here, then?'

'I don't know. But without trust, what is there left?'

The weary smile, the kindly, intelligent eyes, the love of his God beyond reason and the evidence of his senses – he had not changed at all.

In the weeks that followed he was never alone. Every evening after supper he tended the injured, comforted the dying. When word went round the prisoners that he was a priest, several came to him for a prayer or a blessing. In that vile place they went to him as a drowning man clutches at a straw.

Many employers of outside working parties fed their slave labourers adequately. There was no shortage of food outside; rations inside the camp were deliberately punitive. Several prisoners who worked outside the camp would save part of their midday rations and eat them just before they returned to camp. They were searched on their return and punished if they tried to bring anything in. Father Klein kept part of his rations and smuggled them in day after day, giving the food to several prisoners who had become walking skeletons. A friendly guard turned a blind eye when he searched him.

One day the guard fell sick and was replaced by another who did not share his reverence for priests. At evening roll call Father Klein was among those selected for punishment. He was bastinadoed with two hundred strokes on the soles of his feet. When the stick broke a fresh one was used. Four sticks in all were needed to complete the punishment. He cried out occasionally – an awful, long-drawn-out, animal howl.

'You want food?' said the commandant. 'You'll get plenty of it now.'

Father Klein was dragged across the yard to a shit bucket and his face put in it several times. We carried him to the *marotka* and the commandant followed him there. 'See that you don't miss morning roll call,' he shouted.

Albert said, 'With respect, Commandant, he can't walk.'

'Then see he crawls to roll call or all of you die.'

Next morning he crawled on his hands and knees to his place in the line where he was punished again. A placard was placed round his neck saying, 'For this we have to thank our Führer,' and he was made to march upright on his knees. Every time he fell forward he received a kick on his backside and blows with sticks. He developed painful abscesses which grew worse as his punishment continued every day. The deputy commandant stubbed out cigarettes on his skin, which became ulcerous. He endured for five days; then his heart gave out and he died.

'Why? Why him?' I shouted silently to the God he'd trusted. 'The one good man in this lousy stinking world of yours. Are you listening? If you're there, you bloody sadist. You've betrayed him.'

When the work details lined up that first morning after his legs were reduced to stumps, I volunteered for Father Klein's place in the outside working party. By now I had become gaunt and emaciated like one of those reflections from a trick mirror at a fair: all verticals, a seemingly one-dimensional man. Yet I was still taller and stronger than several other prisoners who also wanted his place. I stepped forward, giving a couple of them a hard shove, and was taken on. I was given a donkeyjacket with KT and a white swastika on the back and a yellow arm band with a black swastika. I was taken with the rest of my group to the police headquarters in the town. Our job was to clean every room in the large, square, stone building. The gendarmes worked us hard but did not illtreat us.

I had been at the camp for four months and worked on the outside gang for one week. I've lasted so far, I thought, somehow, in spite of the mad commandant and his weasel deputy, in spite of the fanged guards. I was beginning to feel that life was improving.

The next day I was summoned to the commandant's room and told that I was being transferred to Russia. The Russians were claiming all German soldiers as prisoners-of-war.

30

When I was packed off to Russia in November, my family was still in Waldburg. What happened to them before they too had to move I learned much later.

Liese's baby was born in February. 'For six days she didn't even look at it,' Martha said. 'It was a beautiful child with a round face, completely bald, with no eyebrows and eyelashes so fine you could hardly see them against the pale skin. I fed him with water and sugar but it wasn't enough. He was hungry and cried, and put his little fist in his mouth and sucked and sucked, and cried. *Mein Gott!* I didn't know what to do. Then Max's father said, "If you don't stop that baby crying, we'll all be thrown out onto the street. If you want to murder it, kill it quickly – don't starve it to death."

' "You can't," I shouted, "you promised the priest to look after it." I don't know why I said that. She never told me what was said when he visited her. But I knew she respected him. She'd often said, "He's a man in a million." So I said, "You promised him." And she must have done, because she then began to feed and look after the poor thing – not with any affection, I suppose you can't expect her to, after what happened – but it meant the baby would live.'

Martha's son Franz, who had turned thirteen, and Leo, who was twelve but tall for his age, now lived permanently in the hiding place. The girls, Maria and Erika, remained indoors and accompanied the women into the hiding place in the evening. Only little Dietrich went out of doors, spending all his time on the skis that Max had made him for Christmas.

As if out of nowhere a Czech youth of fifteen blocked Dietrich's path.

'You stole those skis. Hand them over, German shit,' he said.

'I didn't. Uncle Max made them for me.'

'You stole them. Hand them over. I'm a partisan.'

The word 'partisan' terrified Dietrich. A partisan had taken me away to a camp and could take him; the youth looked as big as a man.

'Come on, hand them over.' He grabbed the skis and swaggered away.

Dietrich ran home and refused to step outside for days. Max offered to make another pair of skis for him, but he didn't want them. 'They'll only be taken away again,' he said. He began to have nightmares: they were after him, he said, and he was running, always running, with them hard on his heels, their mouths wide open, their teeth glistening – snapping, howling, galloping after him till it was impossible to tell whether they were partisans or wolves. He became alarmed by footsteps outside the door, by voices on the floor below. During the day, when he was playing with Erika and Maria, half his mind was alert to the slightest sound. He grew pale and thin, a subdued, nervous child who lived in the shadow of fear.

One morning in April Czech gendarmes arrived at the house and demanded to see the German occupants. They brought with them the official notice of expulsion. All Germans from Waldburg were to assemble outside the post office at three o'clock that afternoon. They could take 50 kilos of baggage per person. 'Resettlement' was the official word for kicking people out of their own country. I wonder how the big three of the Potsdam Agreement – Stalin, Churchill and Truman – would like to be 'resettled' elsewhere, preferably with a good hard kick up the backside to get them moving?

Since the agreement was signed the previous summer there had been rumours and counter-rumours about expulsion. In Waldburg they saw the awful columns of German women and children, expelled from Troppau, being force-marched towards the frontier by Czech guards with whips: footsore, hungry, parched with thirst, the babies crying, children whining, the mothers too exhausted to pay much heed in the fierce summer sun. Martha and Liese had given several of them drinks of water before the guards urged them on. How those Czechs loved their whips! News came months later that this sad convoy was turned back at the American border, refused entry because they were in such poor physical condition. The Americans made it plain to the Czechs that they would refuse to accept any further refugees unless they were healthy and reasonably fit. Another batch of expelled Germans taken in similar fashion to the border with East Germany were refused entry on the same grounds. Since that time there had been no forced marches and rumours of expulsion had died down.

Liese and Martha, Max and his father packed hurriedly. Whatever could be fitted into battered suitcases was crammed in; whatever was left over was bundled into sheets tied like enormous Christmas puddings.

At the post office the crowds grew. Dietrich started shaking when he saw the gendarmes; he could not take his eyes off their guns. Their papers were checked and they were put onto lorries.

'Give me your hand, Dietrich,' Max said. 'It's all right. I won't let them harm you.'

The boy stayed close to him like a crumpled bird.

'Here,' said Max, taking out of his pocket a small wooden disc the size of a coin, carved with a ring of oak leaves on one side and a cross on the other. 'You keep this now. It's been with me all the time I was a soldier, seen a lot of battles. It's yours now.'

'But this is your good-luck piece.'

'I want you to have it now.'

'If I have it, won't your good luck go away from you?'

'No, because you'll keep it safe for me. It works for those we love as well.'

The convoy of lorries drove to Muna, where they were taken inside a large shed and asked to open all their baggage for inspection. Every single item was taken out and examined by the guards, who took whatever they wanted, saying they were confiscating it. They took nearly everything: all the raincoats, the single umbrella, a lifejacket that was Leo's prized possession, my box of tools, my mother's shawl that had been given as a wedding present, all the crockery and cutlery except for one spoon which they allowed for each member of my family. Dietrich's teddy bear was slit open and disembowelled, its stuffing searched carefully for jewellery. What was left were old clothes, eiderdowns and some battered saucepans.

A few feet away angry voices were heard. An elderly man with a hernia was ordered to remove the cloth he had strapped round his abdomen. He had hidden his gold watch there. The watch was taken away and the man given a beating.

Their reception camp was an old munition works with railway lines running through it. They walked along these until they came to rows of barracks, with bunk beds, where they were housed. They fed the children with the food they had brought along with them; the rest stayed hungry because no meal was provided that everning or the next morning. Max tried to find out more about the camp from the other inmates who had arrived a few days before them. There were several hundred refugees there, not only from the Sudetenland but also from Hungary and Slovakia. Nobody had any idea how long they were to be kept there or where they were being sent.

'We're fed at midday,' an old man said. 'The guards leave us pretty much to our own devices here. We never see them except at the midday meal. Each family sends one or two people to fetch the food from the kitchen – it's eaten in our barracks. It's always the same: a large pot of watery soup, but with enough bread – enough for that meal and also enough to keep over for the evening and next morning. We won't get fat on it but we won't starve. We wash in the stream outside, ourselves and any clothes.'

They lived there for two weeks. One morning they were told to prepare themselves to leave in the afternoon. A long train consisting of cattle wagons rumbled into the camp. They kept close together, for it was more necessary than ever that they should not be separated now. In the railway carriage they sat on the bare floorboards, on ancient suitcases or bundles of clothes. There were no windows; thin strips of light came through the slats at the sides. At last they were moving. Where to? No one knew.

'To Russia.'

'To Poland.'

'To England.'

'To America.'

'Don't be stupid. We must still be in Czechoslovakia. They'll take us to a concentration camp and finish us off.'

'*Dumpkopf!* They wouldn't have fed us if that's what they intended.'

'*Dumpkopf* yourself! You'll see.'

Max and his father tried to peer through the chinks in the carriage, but saw nothing to give them a clue to their surroundings. Night came on and only the children slept soundly. 'Every time the train stopped,' Liese said, 'I thought, now they'll take us all out, shoot all of us and leave us in the dark. I couldn't sleep. I prayed: Jesus Maria, keep us safe. And you see, they did.'

Through the night and on into the next morning the train went. When it stopped again everybody was ordered out. They were still in Czechoslovakia but near the frontier. Czech guards with rifles were everywhere.

A Czech in army uniform with a great quantity of braid came towards the crowds, accompanied by another man with a loudhailer. The man with the hailer spoke in German.

'Listen carefully. Listen carefully. All children step forward and go with the guards. All adults, stay where you are.'

The children did not move.

'Move! Ask your children to move,' the man with the loudhailer said.

The guards advanced towards the crowds, motioning the children forward with their rifles.

'Leo,' Liese said, 'take Dietrich's hand. Hold hands with Erika, Franz and Maria. Stay together.'

The older children complied, but Dietrich screamed and sobbed and would not part from Max.

'Hush, Dietrich!' Max said. 'You must go with the others. I'll wait here for you. I promise. I won't move one millimetre from here until you return. It won't be long. Do you have the good-luck charm with you? Hold it in your left hand.'

Max handed him over to Leo, and the children were led away by the guards, Dietrich turning round frequently and looking at Max from time to time until they were out of sight.

They were taken, Leo said, into a large shed and asked to line up. Groups of Czech civilians moved along the line, scrutinizing the children's faces. Then officials came round, stopped near each child and spoke to him in Czech, waited for an answer, and spoke again several times, observing the child's responses closely. The questions were repeated in German before the officials moved on to the next child: 'What is your name? Where were you born? Do you speak Czech?'

When the official stood in front of Dietrich, the boy stared at him but could not speak, even when questioned in German.

'Tell him,' Leo said. 'Tell him you were born . . .'

The man stopped him immediately. 'Let him speak for himself. Where were you born?'

He waited but Dietrich did not reply. 'You don't need to be afraid of him.' he said, indicating Leo. 'You can tell me. I'm here to protect you.'

Still no reply.

'Where is your mother?'

'I want my *Mutter*,' Dietrich cried out, 'I want my *Mutter*.'

'Where *is* your mother?'

'Outside.'

'Where is your real mother?'

'Outside. She's waiting for me outside, with Uncle Max.'

'Then you can go to her as soon as you've answered my question. Where were you born?'

'Waldburg.'

The official summoned a guard. 'Take these children back to their mother. Check their papers for Waldburg as their place of birth.'

Liese realized later, from the questions the children repeated, that the Czechs were making sure that no Czech children were being abducted by Germans. They were looking for the missing children of Lidice, the Czech village that had been razed by the SS during the war in reprisal for harbouring the men who had assassinated their commander, Heydrich. Every man and woman in the village had been shot; all the children had been taken away and placed with German families.

31

At last they were allowed to walk through the barriers across the Czech frontier into Germany and, to their great relief, found themselves in the American zone. Unarmed soldiers, except for the sentries – in close-fitting, smart uniforms, casual, unhurried, bursting with health and easy living. A strange army speaking a strange language – the conquerors.

Their papers were examined and they were asked to walk in single file through a barrier. Each person, including the children, was sprinkled liberally with DDT powder in the armpits, on the neck, down the back, and even down trousers or skirt. I wonder what the Americans, who call us *Krauts*, thought of this ragged army as, powdered and deloused, enveloped in a cloud of DDT, it stepped warily onto German soil. They too were far from their homeland, stuck there nearly a year after the war was over, administering the resettlement of refugees, they who came from a land founded largely by refugees. Perhaps it was because of their ancestors that they turned out to be the most generous of the occupying forces.

Every family was given a large pot of soup, a thick, nourishing broth, the kind of food they had not seen for years. They were put onto a waiting train. On and on they rolled for half a day until they arrived at a vast collection camp in the Rhineland where they stayed for three days. Everything here was exceptionally clean. They were housed in wooden huts, fed well and allowed to rest.

They were almost sorry to leave, but move on they must. Now the familiar faces of other families from Waldburg disappeared and their places taken by others, for it was official policy to disperse the inhabitants of each town so that they would not cause trouble by banding together in their new surroundings. Another train and another camp, this time being allowed to stay for one day only.

On the move again to yet another collection camp, where they were greeted by a Bürgermeister and an old priest. The Bürgermeister made a brief speech welcoming them to Hessen; the priest said a short prayer and gave his blessing. The Bürgermeister had a list with the names of all the families assembled there. He read out each name and the name of the place where that family was being sent. Liese and Martha and Max were to go to Wolfstein in the Odenwald.

They arrived by train at Wolfstein, a small village which had become a terminus for the railway since the tunnel that used to take the trains farther on had been blown up by gangs of Ukrainians after the war. The inhabitants of the village, and others from a wide radius covering the surrounding area, were waiting outside the station. Liese thought they were there as a welcoming committee and was moved to think she was lucky enough to come to such warm-hearted people. She was disillusioned very quickly. The faces were not welcoming but surly and resentful. As she learned later, these were the people on whom they were being forcibly billeted by the American authorities. Every house in the area had been checked to see what accommodation was available and whether the varied and often ingenious excuses given for not taking outsiders into their homes were justified.

'We have no room at all.'

'The house is falling to bits and quite dangerous to live in.'

'My mother has nervous spasms and fits when she sees strangers.'

'I wouldn't ask a dog to live the way we do.'

'The roof has fallen in.'

Nearly every house was forced to accommodate the number of refugees decided on by the Bürgermeister and his inspectors. They also had to pay a property tax to help with the resettlement. Small wonder that there were no welcoming banners. The single concession the authorities made over the compulsory billeting was that the host family could choose which refugee families they took into their home. Those assembled outside the railway station had come to make their selection.

They walked around, looking them over like cattle at an auction. Families without children were chosen first. Max and his father were taken by a family in Steinbach.

'I want to go with you,' Dietrich said.

'You must look after your mother. I'll come and see you, I promise.'

Martha, Franz and Maria were taken by a family in Eberhausen.

All that was left now were families with very young children and babies. A girl of fourteen with bold, dark eyes, who had already looked over Liese and the children several times and discussed them with a man old enough to be her grandfather, came towards them again. She looked at Leo and smiled. 'She was making eyes at him,' Liese said.

She looked at Liese and said, 'My mother said I wasn't to bring anyone with a baby. But there isn't much choice now. You can come with me.' She led them to a cart hitched to a cow.

'You can sit in front with me,' she said to Leo.

'Where are we going?'

'To Eberhausen.'

The girl, Magda Kramer, did all the talking; the grandfather sat dourly through the whole journey. The only sound he uttered was a loud honking noise when he blew his nose. Up and up the hill they went, with nothing but fields and woods around them. Eberhausen was a tiny remote village, the houses with sharply pointed roofs, grimy, rundown, badly in need of a facelift. They arrived at a large old farmhouse and waited outside while Magda and her grandfather disappeared indoors for a long time. Magda returned accompanied by her mother, a large, square woman with the same dark eyes and sharp nose. Their faces were flushed as if they had been having a heated argument: Magda peeved and defiant, her mother glowering and suspicious.

'Magda will show you to your room,' she said.

The girl showed them to a room at the top of the house. 'Here we are. I'll leave you to settle in.'

The room was plainly furnished with beds along one wall, a wardrobe and a chest of drawers along another. In the middle was a small square table and four chairs. It had a single window that looked out onto the farm midden, the mixture of dung and straw piled roof high in a large open shed. This was to be their home, and mine, for a long time.

32

The train rumbles and roars eastwards. I, with other German prisoners-of-war, am being taken through the November night like a falling star in the vast wilderness of space. USSR . . . USSR . . . USSR . . . the wheels chant, as we move towards that country, which, sprawling over half a continent, waits with its huge jaws to swallow me up, perhaps for ever, as it has swallowed up whole armies in the war.

We change trains, and two of the prisoners suddenly break ranks and run. They are shot down and no one tries to escape for the rest of the journey. The temperature drops sharply and ice forms on the slats of the cattle wagon. Out of the train at last and blinking in the unaccustomed light as we jolt along in lorries. A landscape ironed flat as far as the eye can see, the cold biting into the bone.

We arrive at last – prisoner-of-war camp at Zaporozhye in the Ukraine. First duty: having our heads shaved. When the last man has been smoothed as a billiard ball, second duty: 'Line up in the yard and remove every stitch of clothing.' While we stand there in freezing weather, turning blue, fingers becoming heavy blocks of ice, our clothes are taken away, deloused and eventually returned.

Third duty: 'You will report to the German unit.'

There seemed to be hundreds of prisoners around in different uniforms: Hungarians, Finns and Japanese, who appear to be the best protected from the cold in heavy quilted jackets with fur-lined hoods. I was looking enviously at the Japanese when I collided with someone walking in the opposite direction.

'Watch where you're going, turnip head,' he said angrily.

'Sorry.'

We looked at each other in disbelief. 'What have they done to you, Martin?' Green eyes and dark hair, the face much thinner but still perfectly proportioned – Gerhard, whom I'd last heard of with the German army in Hungary. Gerhard, who had come visiting us with gifts across the border, the only one among my friends, apart from Max, who was still alive. It was the first time since my arrest that I felt happy – a surge of pure joy, a lifting of the spirit that disregarded and obliterated my surroundings.

'I'm supposed to report to the German unit. Can you take me to them?'

'No, don't go to them, Martin. You'll be finished. They're mostly on the heavy jobs. No, you come with me.'

'But you're German, Gerhard.'

'I'm a lucky German. I'm with the Jewish unit – mainly Jews from Hungary, and quite separate from the Hungarian POWs. Here,' he said, delving into the inner recesses of his coat and handing me a chunk of black bread hidden in his fist. 'It's not much, but it'll help you last out till evening. Keep a tight hold on it. The thieving bastards here will murder their own grandmothers for food.'

The Jewish contingent were dressed in German army uniforms. Three of them were smoking an evil-smelling tobacco wrapped in cones made of newspaper. The others were sprawled on the ground, some propping up each other back to back.

'Lazlo,' Gerhard said to one of them, 'I've brought a friend. He belongs here.'

Lazlo was small and wiry, with dark hair forming a V at the brow, a thin, pale face, and eyes like a fox's, alert and wary.

'Lazlo Gabor, the team leader,' Gerhard said.

'Have you done any painting, plastering or interior decoration?' Lazlo asked.

'No.'

'Never mind. If anyone asks you if you have a trade, you're a skilled interior decorator. I'll fix it with the Work Controller.'

He left to do his fixing.

'He's been here a long time,' Gerhard said. 'He knows the ropes.'

He asked me about the concentration camp.

'The Russians are cleverer than the Czechs,' he said. 'They don't need to beat prisoners to death. They let them die of their own accord, with a little help from starvation rations and hard labour. Each unit has its quota – if you don't fulfil it, you don't eat. The Russians have a saying, "Those who work, eat; those who don't, go to heaven." It's really tough in the hard jobs – shovelling cement, digging foundations for factories, working in the quarry – if hunger doesn't kill, the cold will.'

'You seem to have managed.'

'Yes, but our unit works indoors. And we supplement our rations in other ways. I told you, Lazlo can fix anything.'

'How on earth did the Japanese get here?'

'They're what used to be the Manchurian army. The Russians need men for work. So here they are. They started dying off like flies in the cold because the Russians took away their winter uniforms. One of their officers protested to the commandant; when nothing was done, he committed hara kiri with a razor blade – very messy. But they gave his men back their uniforms.'

'And the Jews? What are they doing here?'

'That was damned unlucky. Towards the end of the war the SS rounded up Jews in Budapest and used them as forced labour, digging tank traps against the advancing Russian army. They took German uniforms off dead soldiers and made the Jews wear them. The Russians conquered the area and – *kaput!* They became prisoners-of-war.'

One of a group of three, introduced as Tibor Kadar, stopped puffing his newspaper cone and came forward. He had a long, grave face with sad eyes. ' "You are our liberators," I said to the Russians, "How can you do this to us? What have we done to you? We're like a salami being sliced from both ends." But it was no good. My mother always said I'd come to a bad end.'

I met some of the other members of the unit: Bela Goldstein, a tall, imposing figure with a supercilious expression heightened by sharply-arched eyebrows, who had been a fashionable portrait painter in Budapest; Bruno Kuhn, who had been a head waiter in a grand hotel and retained a smooth deference acquired from years of conducting well-heeled guests to their tables; Ferenc Schild, a chemist, who spoke very fast, the words trying to keep pace with an inventive, mercurial mind; and the brothers Juri and Janos Fischer, who spent their time arguing with each other but were inseparable.

'How did you get into this unit, Gerhard?'

'They were here before I arrived. I was in civilian clothes when I was taken prisoner. A patriotic Hungarian, damn his eyes, pointed me out to the Russians, who brought me here. I was put to work with the German unit in the quarry. I fell ill and was then assigned to corpse gathering, stripping them of their clothes and slinging the bodies into ditches. That's where Tibor found me. He came with Lazlo to take a couple of greatcoats before the pile of clothes was handed over to the Russians. I'd known him in Budapest – he was my dentist. I was in very poor shape. I'd have died if the Jewish unit hadn't taken me in.'

But there was more to it than that, as Tibor informed me. Gerhard had been the interpreter to the German general in Budapest. For a long time he had been stealing documents from the general's safe; they were death warrants for Hungarian Jews. Gerhard memorized the names and tipped off Tibor, who passed the word to the Jews to move out of the area.

'You live dangerously,' I said.

He shrugged his shoulders. 'A man's a man, Martin.'

This was a side of Gerhard's nature I'd never suspected. Everything had come so easily to him: academic success, a job in a flourishing business, important connections by marriage, an exalted position in the army – all this, and good looks too. And yet he risked losing everything and put his life on the line again and again for people he did not even know. It was as near as I ever came to heroism, a quiet unspectacular kind that did not win medals and sought no rewards.

His wife and children were in Hungary, safe, thanks to his influential father-in-law. He received letters from home regularly and a parcel every two months.

'We can go to our barracks now,' Gerhard said, as the hooter sounded.

The barracks were much larger than those in the Czech camp, with three tiers of bunk beds and separate latrines.

'Don't you work on Sundays?' I asked.

'Yes, but today is an officially recognized, Soviet-authorized Sunday. We're given one from time to time. It means we can do what we like after lunch. This morning we had to clean out our barracks. We went on a bug hunt in the mattresses. I caught twenty-eight; Bruno got eighty-two. On other official Sundays we have a personal delousing session: all hair shaved off, armpits as well, and stand around naked till our clothes are returned from the steam room. Sometimes we're turned out of the barracks and hang about for hours until they're given a random search. Some Sunday mornings are devoted wholly to political indoctrination classes. It all depends on what the Russians feel like. Sometimes the officers organize a camp concert with volunteers from different groups.'

'Where are the officers? I haven't seen any about.'

'They're housed separately from men in the ranks.'

Raised voices were heard from the bunks occupied by Juri and Janos.

'The filthy thieving swine!' Juri said. 'The bread's gone again.'

'It must be rats.'

'Damn it, there were no rats here after this morning's clean-up. It's a two-legged rat.'

Juri called us over to his bunk, which was right on top. 'Look! We'd tied our bags on a string between the bunks. Rats can't possibly run along this. But see! Empty. Both of them,' he said, turning the cloth bags inside out.

'It must have been taken this morning,' Janos said.

I wondered whether the bread Gerhard had given me was stolen from here. I learned that bread had been stolen from this hut for a number of weeks. The thief was clever: the last time he had cut a hole in the mattress and scattered crumbs around it, so that they had assumed it was rats after all.

Lazlo appeared, looking much fatter than when I had last seen him. He took off his coat, removed another coat and quilted jacket, which he handed to me with a cap. 'Put these on if you want to live through the winter.'

'Thank you. How on earth did you . . .'

He raised his hand in warning. 'The only rule to be observed in this unit: take what you're given or refuse it, but don't ask any questions.'

Janos brought the empty bread bags to him. Lazlo's thin pale face looked pinched with anger. 'Bruno's received a parcel today,' he said. 'We'll stay here when you go for the evening meal. We'll bait a trap and see if we can't catch our rat.'

'Darling,' said Bela Goldstein, who called everyone 'darling', 'who's going to have your soup?'

'You have it,' Lazlo said to me.

'Tibor can have mine,' Bruno said.

Bela looked disdainfully over their heads and walked away.

When the hooter sounded for the evening meal we crowded into the canteen barracks, pushing and elbowing our way to a table. We waited, closely packed on benches, while Juri and Janos went to the hatch for food. They returned with bowls of watery soup and small pieces of black bread.

'He wanted to give thirteen only, as usual,' Juri said. 'He had Martin's name on the list but wouldn't give up the fourteenth bowl until he'd consulted the supervisor, who had to consult *his* list.'

I found a piece of unidentifiable vegetable at the bottom of my soup; there were two pieces at the bottom of Lazlo's bowl. The extra portions of bread were handed over to Lazlo and Bruno when we returned to our barracks.

'We caught the swine,' Bruno said, rubbing the knuckles of his huge fist.

They had left the parcel awkwardly concealed under the mattress as if it had been pushed there in a hurry. They had hidden, Lazlo at one door, Bruno at another, and watched the thief as he found the parcel and stuffed most of the contents inside his coat. He was about to leave the hut when they jumped him. They gagged him and worked him over.

'Who was it?'

'A Japanese.'

'They don't all look alike now,' Lazlo said.

Bruno's parcel was shared out. The routine for parcels was always the same. A large part of the contents was given to the guard who opened it for inspection; it was better to give him a share than have him confiscate the whole. The owner then distributed it among the rest of us as he pleased, it being accepted that he should have the lion's share. That day we had a cut of cheese, a slice of salami, and bread made of real flour – it did not go far between fourteen men but it tasted like a feast.

33

Next morning we were turned out of the huts at five o'clock. We went to the canteen barracks where we were given bread and soup similar to the one we had had the previous evening, except that the debris at the bottom was slightly thicker. I found two small pieces of potato and, to my great surprise, a tiny fish the size of my little finger. It was very salty but I ate it – head, tail, fins, bones and all.

Then came the long, long wait outside until the camp gates were opened. We were counted three times and marched out under heavy guard, trudging for threequarters of an hour until we came to what looked like a large building site where the different units went in different directions.

'They're rebuilding a vast industrial complex here,' Gerhard said, 'power stations, hydroelectric works, factories, aluminium smelters and God knows what else.'

Our unit went to a huge barn of a building which, from the outside, was indistinguishable from a factory. It was the new Soviet Hall of Culture, with a large auditorium and stage forming the main part of the building and corridors leading to what was to be an art gallery, a sculpture hall and various committee rooms.

'Darling,' Bela Goldstein said, 'look at it! The triumph of matter over mind. The stark, functional ugliness of the design has, I must confess, a certain brutal impact. Can you feel it? Like entering a vast public lavatory. Too shameful for words.'

Bela's opinions were always extreme, calculated to shock or startle. It was part of the pose of artistic sensitivity he had cultivated, which accounted for much of his popularity as a portrait painter in avant-garde and pseudo-artistic circles. It was a pose that had become a second skin to him, and not even the rigours of life in a POW camp could make him slough it off. In Budapest his reception room was painted with Chinese dragons in whose mouths he placed incense which was lit just before a client arrived for a sitting. Here he was painting the walls in preparation for his murals which, as yet, had not been approved by the Soviet Arts Committee.

'They don't want lovely dragons and heraldic beasts, darling. Nothing abstract or fabulous. Just straightforward, down-to-earth pictures of 'common people engaged in common tasks, but with a sense of purpose and pride in achievement,' they said. So I tossed off a series of poster art sketches, darling, square-jawed, muscular men and granite-faced, muscular women, positively radiating dedication as they gaze fixedly at a rising sun spreading pink and gold on a distant horizon. Kitsch as I could make it. I'm sure they'll approve.'

'If that's what they want, that's what you'll give them,' Lazlo said. 'Otherwise they'll find another team to do this job and we'll be pushing cement or laying bricks.'

Bela muttered something under his breath and settled to work, with Juri and Janos helping him. They had lit the stove, ostensibly to dry out the plaster, and the air, which consisted of slabs of ice when we entered the building, began to thaw to a more bearable temperature. Lazlo worked with Bruno and five others on the area near the stage; he was a trained interior decorator. Tibor, Ferenc, Gerhard and I worked on the frieze that was to run all the way round the inside of the building. I learned how to cast plaster in moulds, several sets at a time, and, as one set dried, to fit another into place. It was skilled, intricate work, making sure the finished product did not crack.

Long before the midday hooter sounded I had my ears cocked for it. At the first blast we downed tools and hurried to the central canteen, a huge barn of a building, newly built. Tibor and Ferenc brought the food from the hatch: no bread, but bowls of *kasha*, a mash of a little buckwheat and barley, with ground acorns, horse chestnuts and anything else available, boiled in salted hot water.

It was more substantial than the soup served morning and evening in the camp canteen, which was so acidic that it corroded the bowls it came in and produced a raging thirst.

Instead of joining the rest of us sitting round the stove in the Hall of Culture, Lazlo and Gerhard disappeared after the meal. They returned just before the hooter sounded the resumption of work. They handed two bars of hard, rough soap to Ferenc. While Tibor, Gerhard and I continued working on the frieze, Ferenc worked on the soap. He melted it down, perfumed it with crushed herbs, and recast it into fancy shapes in some of the smaller moulds from the frieze. The tablets of soap were handed over to Lazlo, who removed a floorboard under the stage and stowed them.

The next day, after lunch, Lazlo and Gerhard exchanged the soap for food from Russian civilians who also worked in gangs in the area; the women prized the scented soap so highly that the demand for it remained insatiable. They gave us what we needed most of all: food, of which they themselves were very short. Silver and gold were worthless here; you can't eat metal. It was the food received from this trade that kept the team of Hungarian Jews alive. We gave them scented soap; they gave us bread, potatoes or *machorka*, which consisted of chopped-up stalks of the tobacco plant. We roasted the potatoes on the stove and devoured them, skin and all. For those of us who did not smoke, the *machorka* became a form of currency in the camp. It was amazing how many POWs preferred to give up their scanty bread ration rather than do without a smoke. One man in particular, a tall, skeletal German, who was called Hunger Pastor because of his craving for tobacco, was always hanging around the latrines, trying to cadge a smoke. He begged, whined, threatened, bought; he would have sold his soul for a smoke if anyone had thought it worth buying. It was a wonder that he stayed alive.

In the evening the hooter sounded to knock off work at five o'clock. We had to line up to be searched and waited for the count, numbers checked and rechecked three times. The long walk back under guard, the prospect of soup and bread working like a magnet, and eventually the bunk – dead to the bugs, to the cold, to everything – to dream of one hot roast potato sizzling and growing larger and larger until it filled the whole room.

The pattern of life in camp became routine. When some of the old moulds became worn out Tibor suggested that I should try to make different shapes for the new ones. I found working with clay similar to working with yeast dough at the bakery, only the clay was more malleable and gave greater control over the finished product.

Although the demand for fancy soaps was constant, the number that could be turned out within the time allotted for our work quota was limited. Food became an obsession. Even with the supplements I was always hungry. But hunger had its compensations.

'See you don't eat too much,' Gerhard said.

'Chance would be a fine thing.'

'I'm serious. The camp doctors inspect us at regular intervals, and pinch the flesh on arms and sides. If they think you've enough there, they send you to the quarry.'

Outside the camp huge mountains of grain, guarded by soldiers, stood rotting in the rain. Neither the POWs, nor their guards, who were also short of food, nor Russian civilians, were allowed to go near them. The farmers had been ordered to pile up the grain, but there was no transport to shift it to areas of distribution, so it stayed there month after month, providing food for rats.

34

At Zaporozhye the seasons turned around to another winter and another summer. Gerhard brought me news that my family was in Eberhausen. The war had been over for two years and still the Russians showed no sign of wanting to release their POWs.

'They have a vast building programme and not enough labour,' Gerhard said. 'If they let us go, who's going to build their factories and industrial estates?'

By now work on the main part of the Soviet Hall of Culture was complete. Further work was suspended until the Jewish unit fulfilled a top priority: making a gigantic aluminium statue of Lenin which was to be placed in the centre of the town. Factory premises in the last stages of completion were commandeered for the purpose, several photographs of Lenin provided, and the project began.

Lazlo gave the photographs to Bela. 'See if you can make a clay model to resemble these.'

'I'm a portrait painter, darling, not a sculptor, and certainly not someone who works in clay.'

'Martin knows all about clay. Get him to help you.'

The models I had made for the frieze in the Hall of Culture had been much admired, but I had never made a figure before. After several attempts at trial and error, it began to take shape. The body and the stance were relatively easy but the face was difficult. I don't think his most ardent devotees could have gazed at Lenin's face for so long or with as much attention as we did. Eventually we got him, and waited for him to dry out.

Tibor, the dentist, and Ferenc, the chemist, organized Lenin's transformation. He was placed in a container and plaster-of-Paris poured round him. As the plaster dried, he underwent a sex change.

'Lenin in drag, darling,' Bela said. 'Did he have such tendencies, do you think?'

The female plaster mould was removed very carefully (one slip now and all the work would have to be done again) and coated with shellac on the inside. The mould was closed, leaving a small hole at the top through which plaster-of-Paris was poured until the cavity was filled completely.

'Lenin's sex returned to him, darling. He needs it like a hole in the head,' Bela said.

Once the plaster had set, the casing of the female mould was removed and there he stood, all sixty centimetres of him, in characteristic oratorical stance, pure white, the father of the nation he had led in bloody revolution.

'It's good,' Tibor said.

'It's damned good,' Ferenc said.

'Yes, darling,' Bela said, 'it will do. I can't say I *like* it as art, but it'll do. It has a definite vulgar appeal. Its monster version in aluminium should be horrendously popular.'

It was approved by the Arts Committee and Lenin was on his way to greatness. The plaster model was scaled up to a larger-than-life-size replica in wax. We built a box around it and packed it with clay, completely encasing the wax figure except for a small opening at the top. When the clay hardened the most difficult and hazardous part of the project began: very slowly, very carefully, white-hot molten aluminium was poured into the opening until it filled the clay mould completely, melting and displacing the wax.

'If we foul this up,' Lazlo said, 'we're for the quarry.'

Lenin hardened his heart. His clay covering was removed and he stood in solid aluminium, dull and tarnished for the moment, but intact. We shouted with relief and congratulated each other and danced round him in wild abandon. The Russian guards came running but did not intervene. We examined every part of him, smoothed away rough edges, massaged and polished and buffed until he shone with benevolence – caring, persuasive, intense, dedicated – a politician to his silver fingertips.

The statue was to be unveiled at a public ceremony in the town. A public holiday was declared and the inhabitants of Zaporozhye ordered to attend. All the members of the Arts Committee were there, with civic dignitaries weighted with their medals and a sense of their own importance. We were the only POWs allowed to be present at the ceremony. After the long speeches and obligatory clapping, the patriotic songs and patriotic smiles, so many and so fixed that Lenin should have melted with boredom, at last the statue was unveiled. For all I know it is standing there to this day, glinting in the sun, a man with a metallic heart, symbol of the new Russia let loose after Czarist imperialism.

The next day Lazlo brought amazing news. 'The Arts Committee and local government officials are so pleased with our statue that they've offered us a permanent home in Russia. They need our skills. We can send for our families – as soon as they join us we'll be housed in flats in the town.'

'And if we don't?' Tibor said.

'We'll remain POWs.'

'The supreme accolade,' Gerhard said, 'a permanent home in the workers' paradise which no worker is allowed to leave.'

'Think of it, darling,' Bela said, 'international fame at last – producing millions of little replicas of Lenin.'

'This means they've no intention of letting any prisoners return, ever,' Gerhard said. 'They need people like us for skilled work, and labourers for building roads and factories. They just don't have enough people. They'll never let us go.'

'We'll have to escape,' Tibor said.

'Impossible,' Lazlo said. 'We can get out of the camp easily enough, but we'd be caught almost as soon as we left. There's no transport; only Gerhard has enough Russian to be able to get by and the country's dead flat in every direction. The only way you'll get out is by lopping off an arm or leg or getting TB, some form of permanent disability. The Russians will send you back to your family then. I'm staying where I am. We're POWs – they'll *have* to send us home some time.'

That seemed to be the general opinion.

'If anyone thinks he can escape he must take his chance and go,' Lazlo said. 'But don't expect a team effort. I don't believe in suicide.'

Lazlo knew more about camp life than anyone else. If he said escape was impossible, then it was. And yet I could not stop thinking about it. I had no wish to become a permanent member of the workers' paradise. I am my own man; I don't want perfection. I'll settle for less grandiose, more selfish goals: a little room to breathe, enough food in my belly, and sufficient money to support my family and indulge my vices. Ever since Gerhard had brought me news of my family's whereabouts I had begun to think about them. I wanted to see the children again and even Liese with her sharp tongue and abrasive ways, for whom I felt pity tinged with affection. It was her tragedy always to do the wrong thing with the best motives in the world. So much goodness is difficult to live with. But here the difficulties faded with distance. I remembered mostly how hard she worked, how selfless she was with the children and, in marrying me, how strange and disappointing a bargain she made for herself. She wanted to change me, make me a better man, and, goodness knows, there's room for improvement. It was her misfortune too to be tied to someone who did not want to change. We rubbed along, chafing each other's skin, like rough woollen clothes to which familiarity had given the semblance of comfort, which neither wanted to discard to be left out in the cold.

35

We were back at work in the Soviet Hall of Culture. A chandelier which had been found in the wreckage of a shelled building was to be hung in the auditorium. We spent the day cleaning and assembling it. It had to be in place before the end of the day. Juri and Janos fixed it to the ceiling. It was almost time for the evening hooter and we were clearing up hurriedly.

'Can you lend us a hand, Martin?' Juri called, as Janos and he carried the ladders away.

I came over and was picking up the tools from the floor when I felt my head burst open. I was drowning in a roaring tinkling waterfall of glass.

I was swimming underground in a long, dark passage which seemed to be made of treacle. From the far end came a booming echo: 'Permanent disability . . . permanent disability.' I surfaced into consciousness. I had a massive headache and my head felt four times its normal size; I raised an exploratory hand and found that my head was swathed in bandages. My right shoulder and upper arm were also bandaged. I wiggled my toes. I had taken quite a crack but wasn't paralysed. I looked about me – lines of beds on either side, sharp sunlight slanting from a row of windows on the opposite wall, the stinging smell of disinfectant – I was in the camp hospital. I found it more restful to keep my eyes closed. 'Permanent disability . . . permanent disability . . .' the words kept going round and round, and brought with them the key to my escape. A blind man is even more useless than a man without an arm or leg. If I could convince the Russians that I was blind they would have to let me go.

I heard German voices.

'Is he dead yet?'

'No, still breathing.'

'He's done for. In a coma for fifteen hours – he won't come round.'

'They'll finish him off with an injection, then.'

I lay still for a while. When the voices faded, I called feebly, 'Is anyone around? Where am I?'

The patient in the next bed raised himself on his elbow and said, 'You're all right. You're in the hospital. The doctor will come round to see us soon.'

'The doctor comes at night?'

'It's not night, it's a bright sunny morning.'

'Bright . . . sunny . . . Oh God! I'm blind. I can't see a thing.' I put on quite a performance, shouting and crying, 'I'm blind, I'm blind. God help me, I'm blind.'

Several of the patients expressed their concern and tried to console me. When the woman doctor came I put on another performance for her benefit. She was a tough audience, brusque and uncommunicative. Every day she came, tall, square-jawed, built like a man, and although I modified my performance to quiet despair and then to hopeless acceptance, she was still unconvinced.

The sledgehammer in my head stopped and the last of my bandages was taken off, but I could see from the frown on the doctor's face that she was unconverted. She devised a series of tests to catch me out. It was now a battle of wits and willpower. She moved her hand rapidly from side to side in front of my face to see if I would follow it with my eyes. I'm blind, I said to myself, and looked straight ahead. She brought Lazlo in to see me and stood a short distance behind me to observe my reactions. I suspected a trap and behaved accordingly. It was difficult to know whether Lazlo was taken in or not. The doctor kept food in front of me and kept me sitting for hours under observation. Hungry as I was, I forced myself not to reach out and take it. I fixed my gaze at a point just above the food in order to stop salivating. She took me into a room that led into another down three steps. She walked silently down the steps, stood at the far end and said, 'Come over here.' Don't hesitate, walk straight on, I said to myself. I did, and fell down the steps in a heap. She lit a candle and brought it quite near my eyes; I willed myself not to shift my gaze or flinch. She took me to a room where a thread was stretched from wall to wall at eye level and asked me to walk across the room. I walked straight into the thread and cried out when it cut into my eyes.

The other patients in the ward had been convinced of my blindness a long time ago. Harder to bear than all the tests was the ordeal of having to lie in bed and watch them steal my bread ration. I was ravenous but could do nothing. They became bolder and, instead of moving stealthily, stood in front of me, stole my food and ate it as I watched.

I grew thinner than I had ever been but my gaunt appearance worked in my favour. When the Russians eventually ran out of tests, my emaciated condition combined with my blindness to persuade them to send me to Germany. I was obviously incapable of any work. My relatives could have the burden of looking after me.

36

In the summer of 1947 I arrived in Germany – a foreign land occupied by foreigners. The American soldiers were so healthy it hurt to look at them. They sent me to a hospital to recuperate and, as I no longer needed to feign blindness, it was there that I saw myself in a mirror for the first time in years. I nearly frightened myself to death. A freak stared back at me, with sunken eyes rimmed with owlish dark circles, a long, diagonal scar across the forehead, a pinched hollow-cheeked face over which the skin was drawn tight, the head close-shaved, making it look even more like a skull. I'm not surprised the Americans at the border thought I was round the twist.

I was in no hurry to leave the hospital, where all I had to do was rest and eat. I kept inventing various aches and pains, but eventually I was discharged, given my ticket to Wolfstein and arrived at Eberhausen. Eberhausen. What a hole of a place in the back of beyond! Dilapidated, weather-beaten, storm-tossed buildings, a general sense of apathy and decay, the kind of place where even a dog would not bestir itself to scratch its fleas. I passed smallholdings which the owners call 'farms', a sagging village store, a gloomy church, and came to the place where my family lived. Scraggy chickens scratched around in the yard, a sow grunted in her mucky pen, a patient cow chewed the cud in her stall, flicking her ears to dislodge swarms of flies that came from the steaming midden behind the house. The house was large, brick-built, faced with wooden shingles that had once been green but now – chipped, broken, rotting with weather and neglect – formed a grey-brown rash disfigured by gaps. A flight of stone steps with an iron rail led to the ground floor, which was raised well above the level of the road. Dark wooden shutters on narrow windows heightened the effect of a building that was dying through neglect. A sharply pointed roof gave it a pinched, severe appearance. It was an unwelcoming place that acquired its atmosphere from its owners.

'What do you want?' said a blowsy, sharp-nosed woman, who, I learned later, was Frau Kramer, the mother of the dark-eyed minx Magda.

'I'm looking for my family, Liese Bron and the children.'

She stared at me as if trying to work out whether I would abscond with the furniture. 'Upstairs,' she said, 'right at the top.'

Liese made a great fuss of me. She looked much older: her hair was duller, flat, straw-coloured, streaked with grey, but still worn in two tight braids wound round her head; her face thinner, lines round the mouth and forehead. The children had changed a good deal. Leo, now thirteen, was almost at my shoulder, all arms and legs, with an open countenance and an easygoing, cheerful temperament; Erika, though a year younger, behaved as if she were much older, a graceful, dreamy child, who would grow into a very attractive adolescent; Dietrich, at nine, was a pale, withdrawn, moody boy, at first wary of me and then clinging. The baby, who was christened Johann, was a handsome, lively toddler, brown-haired, brown-eyed, with an engaging, mischievous smile. Liese had accepted him but always, as I saw her with him, as if a part of her nature held back. The spontaneity and warmth she had shown to our own children at that age were missing. Johann did not seem to mind, and Erika doted on him.

They had lived from hand to mouth. One by one Liese had sold the few household possessions they had brought with them: the battered suitcases, all my clothes except for one pair of trousers and a shirt, all her clothes except the ones she wore and one other set, all but two pots and pans. The money she got for them had very little value and she was cheated over the sales by those who exploited her ignorance. Liese and Martha had smuggled in their wedding rings past the Czech guards by sewing them into their bodices. Liese sold everything else rather than part with her ring. 'It was blessed in church,' she said. 'It was special.' But eventually that too had to go when they were desperate for food, sold to a farmer in exchange for a bag of potatoes.

Max came occasionally, walking from Steinbach on the short cut through the woods, about an hour away. His father was dead and his own health deteriorating. He carved wooden plates and bowls, and just managed to get by. Martha and her children lived in Eberhausen at the other end of the village. Martha too had been selling her belongings in order to exist. 'She went all the way to the River Neckar,' Liese said, 'for a bucket of engine oil which she heard was available from a bombed ship wrecked in the river. She brought it home and cooked potatoes in it but the oil made the food inedible. Rather than throw the potatoes away, she washed them several times in hot water, mashed them up and made a soup. Her children wouldn't touch it because they said it stank. But Martha ate it and was quite sick afterwards.'

The children were better-fed than the adults because the Americans introduced a nourishing midday meal for all children in school. Leo and Erika, with Martha's Franz and Maria, went to Michelberg, seven kilometres away, to the disused railway station that served as a secondary school. Walking there was easy because it was all downhill, but the journey back, especially in the boiling summer, was very tiring. Dietrich's primary school was in the village itself.

The only people in Eberhausen who have enough food are the farmers, and they couldn't care less whether the rest of us live or die. The Kramers, in whose house we are billeted, have two cows, one sow, a few chickens and a smallholding on which they grow wheat. They also have a disused quarry. I asked Frau Kramer if there was any work I could do for her. She looked at me as if I'd crawled out of the nearest drain.

'There's no work here. None at all.'

I swore at her under my breath and walked on. I tried every farm in the village and in the outlying areas. The answer was always the same. There was nothing for it but to beg for food. Once again I went the rounds of the farms, and again, invariably, the answer sent me packing.

'We have no food to spare,' Frau Kramer said, grasping a large pail of frothing milk in both hands, while her chickens scratched around about our feet and her sow could be heard grunting. It is small wonder that farmers are the most hated people in this village. If ever this sleepy place awakens into murderous action, the first victim will be a farmer.

That night I went out to the fields with a pair of scissors and snipped off the tops of the growing wheat. We had porridge the next morning and for many mornings after that, though I never told Liese where I got the grain from. The children gathered beechnuts from the woods, and windfall apples (to which I added several with my own method of gathering); these were grated and cooked with the grain to make a quite edible mash.

Winter was coming on and if we were to live through it I had to find some means of earning a livelihood. About the only thing money could buy cheaply was a railway ticket. I decided it was time I tried my luck in a big city.

I went to Frankfurt, pockmarked by bombs, its centre a vast crater with the rubble of shattered buildings, its streets grey with dirt and devastation. Every dustbin I passed had its human scavengers picking through the revolting contents for anything remotely edible. Two men, who looked like tramps, were fighting over a heap of potato peelings. At every pile of bomb debris, scattered, isolated figures were turning over the bricks, searching for something they never found. I thought that we who lived in the country had a hard time, but here, looking at this grey, scarred cityscape, I realized how much better off we were. We were hungry but got by – just; these people lived like rats in a sewer.

I moved to the back alleys and side streets which had escaped bomb damage. American GIs walked about with the casual assurance of conquerors. We had no GIs in Eberhausen. Looking at them here, I was convinced that America was a land of fabulous wealth with everyone rolling in money, for I have never seen a single poor or hungry GI, not even among the black ones. They were all sleek, smart, well fed, well dressed – they made even the spivs and pimps around, who could afford to wear better clothes than the rest of us, look shabby. Here a black market was flourishing in goods only they could provide: cigarettes, coffee, flour, sugar, chocolate, tinned condensed milk.

This was the sleazy part of the city, rows of decrepit houses packed close together, propping each other up, with shops at street level, where most business was done under the counter, and dark passageways leading upstairs, where money changed hands and no questions were asked. All along this street women of assorted ages, their faces plastered with garish make-up, their clothes tight-fitting and revealing, loitered with obvious intent. Some walked up and down with a seductive swing of the hips, some stood propping up doorways, their brightly painted faces sagging, their eyes restless and predatory; others, invariably the very young, stood in small groups of two or three having loud animated conversations with much forced laughter, trying to draw attention to themselves. The effect was macabre, like watching corpses dancing at their own funeral.

I followed several GIs and picked up their half-smoked cigarettes off the ground, stubbing them out quickly. I collected a number of stubs, and on one occasion a GI who saw me swoop down on a butt, a large Negro with very white teeth and small ears, threw me his half-empty packet. There was always a market for tobacco. Five whole cigarettes and a collection of butts – I had made a small beginning.

Over the next two days I collected more cigarette butts, but it was a business whose profits depended on chance. No one else threw me a half-full packet, and although the stubs enabled us to eat, I knew that they would not tide us through the winter. I decided to expand my interests, diversify my resources, ride with a free market economy and let the forces of supply and demand work to my advantage. You see how easy it is to pick up the jargon of politicians and business tycoons, and how impressive it sounds, when all it means is that I decided on another way of making a fast buck. Here, in this city, there are too many women, too few men, except for the GIs. There is no work available, but there is opportunity for private enterprise. If supply and demand can be brought together, I thought, a living of sorts might be made.

I approached a few of the gaudy women hanging around, who lost interest when they realized I wasn't a client, but regained it when they found I was a pimp. I learned that many of them came in for the day by train, as I had done. These were no good to me. I needed someone familiar with Frankfurt who could put me in touch with the owner of a room for hire. At last I found her: Annemarie, who looked around thirty, a brassy blonde with a loud, throaty laugh. She knew someone who knew someone who had a room to spare.

'It'll cost you,' she said, 'but then doesn't everything these days?'

If I found her a GI ('I don't mind how many, duckie'), she would find me the room.

'Do you mind if they're black?'

She threw back her head and laughed. 'You find 'em, I'll have 'em. Meet me tomorrow, same time, same place. Bring a customer with you.'

Which was how Annemarie and I set up in business. I was paid by the GIs in cigarettes – whole packs of them, not the stubs I'd collected earlier. These were worth their weight in gold, were in fact better than gold, which you couldn't eat here any more than you could in Russia. I sold the cigarettes on the black market or bartered them for food. Annemarie was paid in food: chocolates, coffee, flour, sugar. Her father and husband had been killed in the war; she was supporting her mother and younger brother and sister.

'Does your mother know what you do for a living?' I asked.

'Of course not. She thinks I give German lessons to the Americans. Which I do.' Again she laughed, a laugh of immense vitality, a full, rich sound that promised comfort. 'Does your wife know?'

'Certainly not. She thinks I do business with cigarettes. Which I do, of course.'

I liked Annemarie, her lack of pretensions, her common sense, her ability to look on the funny side in such dismal surroundings, her warm heart and shrewd business brain.

'They talk to me, Martin, afterwards,' she said. 'You wouldn't expect it, would you? But they do. They're homesick, most of them, poor things. They talk of their sweethearts, their friends, even their wives. All they want really is a kiss and a cuddle.'

37

Through Annemarie I met Klaus Buchmann, Herr Baron as he liked to be called. I had taken Annemarie for a drink to my usual bar in Frankfurt, which was more crowded than ever that evening. A jukebox throbbed in a corner, wailing a message from the Andrews Sisters into the smoke-wreathed air:

> You gotta accen-tuate the positive,
> Eee-lee-me-nate the negative,
> Laitch aan to the a-firm-ative,
> Don't put the Mister in between.

Through the smoke a figure appeared at our table. He was about fifty, tall, debonair, with slicked-down, dark hair touched with silver at the temples. He had a dapper, toothbrush moustache in a weasel-like face, which ended in a pointed chin. He was dressed flashily in a loud-checked suit, with patent-leather shoes, and carried in his hand a wide-brimmed Homburg which he kept twirling around.

'Annemarie,' he said, '*Servus!*'

It was a greeting I had not heard (except from Max and Martha) since I'd left the Sudetenland. It is only used with those one knows well. It can mean 'hello' or 'goodbye'.

'Herr Baron . . . Herr Martin Bron,' Annemarie said.

I learned later that the title was a courtesy one, given to the Baron by himself.

'May I join you?' he said, and ordered a round of drinks. He chatted easily, pleasantly. 'Where are you from, Herr Bron? Your accent is familiar.'

'From Waldburg, in the Sudetenland.'

'I knew it,' he said. 'A compatriot. It's a small world. This calls for a celebration.'

He ordered a bottle of expensive Sekt and we toasted each other, exchanging information about the Sudetenland. He came from the same area as I did, from Neustadt, a town somewhat larger than Waldburg. He had lost his accent – I could only detect the faintest trace – for he had left the Sudetenland in 1939 when he joined the army, and had never returned. He had no family left now: his brothers had died on the Russian front, his parents died when Neustadt came under Czech occupation.

'It's time for another bottle,' he said.

'Not for me,' Annemarie said, 'I must be off.'

The Baron and I sat drinking far into the evening, the first of many such evenings, two exiles in a new country, bound together by a long-lost homeland. Whenever I met him, he insisted on paying for the drinks.

'You have a family to support,' he said, 'I have only myself. I can afford to be generous. Why should you grudge me the pleasure?'

And he did take great pleasure in his generosity, which also took the form of presents for Liese and the children: a pair of nylons, coffee, chocolates, tinned milk, eggs and tinned American bacon.

He had been a quartermaster in the army and amassed a tidy sum by selling army stores at black-market prices.

'The army's been good to me,' he said. 'I had a bit of capital put by when the war ended.' He winked slyly. 'I was decorated for keeping the stores in good order.'

That first day I met him he said, 'I could put work your way. What are you willing to do?'

'Anything.'

'Absolutely anything?'

'Absolutely.'

'I have a building I'm converting into a ceramics factory. Can you make cups, saucers, mugs, that sort of thing?'

'Yes.' No point telling him I had not made any. If I could make friezes and Lenin, I could easily make a mug.

'Can you bring me some of your products?' he asked.

'I could make you a plaster mould but I've no kiln to fire it.'

'No problem. Let me have it. I'll have it finished for you.'

Clay and plaster-of-Paris were readily available. I made a plaster mould of a mug and he paid me a good price for it. He stamped them out by the dozen and made a whacking profit. From then on I sold to him on a regular basis.

The Baron was an entrepreneur on a grand scale. Everything he touched turned to gold. He owned (among other things) a large number of slot machines. He supplied the American army with Leica cameras, Zeiss binoculars, microscopes which mysteriously appeared, and even a set of optical instruments which had gone missing from the local hospital. He took me under his wing. We became drinking companions and went gambling together. We never went to grand places; he came to the low dives I frequented where the stakes were within my means.

'You and a hundred others, Martin, give the GIs girls,' he said. 'Sure, they want girls. But that's small-time. You won't make your fortune pimping for them.'

'I won't starve either.'

'Goddammit! You must think big, Martin. When you work with me you're in the big league. It's a totally different ball game. You understand?' He had picked up American slang and flaunted it to show his special relationship with the GIs. 'You and I, Martin, we'll buy and sell cigarettes but we'll smoke cigars. OK?' he said, pulling out two Havanas from his pocket and offering me one.

I don't smoke but I took the cigar, saying, 'I'll keep it for later.'

'OK,' he said, and I knew from his sharp, amused glance that he knew I intended to sell it.

I grew to like and trust the Baron. He had enthusiasm, a quality I had not seen for a very long time and which I thought I had left behind forever. In this rotting, crumbling, broken world in which we exist from day to day, he moved with assurance: cheerful, hopeful, full of plans. He was working for a future while I, like everyone else, was desperately trying to claw my way out of the past. His enthusiasm was infectious. For the first time after so many years, hope appeared: frail, exhausted, tentative, but possible. Every time I met the Baron it grew stronger. I looked forward to our meetings not merely because they were financially rewarding but because I grew to think of him as a friend. I, who had lost all my friends, even Max, who had not survived the winter, found another, all the dearer because he was from the old country.

What with the plaster moulds and pimping (which I had not abandoned in spite of the Baron) and black marketeering, by the time the summer of 1948 came around I wasn't doing too badly. The Baron's factory premises were ready.

'We're all set,' he said. 'I've managed to get hold of two large kilns. It's like this.' He smoothed down his already smooth dark hair that gleamed with brilliantine. 'I have the factory and the equipment, you have the technical expertise. We trust each other. You can be responsible for the technical side, I'll deal with the business end. What do you say to a partnership in the factory? Ten per cent of the profits. How about it?'

'A partnership of ninety to ten? I do all the work and you take all the profit, Klaus?'

'Ten per cent's not a bad share. It'll be a fortune compared to what you make at the moment. I've spent a lot of money on premises and equipment. I need to recoup that and then make a profit.'

'Make it eighty–twenty and I'll come in with you. You can afford to be generous.'

He said nothing but twirled his Homburg round and round in his hand. Then he laughed out loud. 'Goddammit! You're a tough cookie, Martin. But since we're friends, OK. I'll have the papers drawn up for signature. Let's drink to it.'

We sat over our drinks for a long time as he unfolded the plans for the factory. 'We'll begin with pottery and, once our market is captured, turn to fine porcelain. We'll place our ceramics in every home in Frankfurt and then expand to the rest of Germany. After that, who knows? We could well go for the international market, show these Amerikaner what German craftsmanship can do. We're going places, Martin, you and I.'

I was feeling very pleased with myself and my dreams of prosperity. I was moving up in the world. A business of my own, with the Baron's assets in wheeling and dealing, his range of contacts . . . There was no limit to what could be done.

That evening we had a celebration at home. In the middle of the festivities Annemarie walked in. She had no idea what a sensation she caused in the village or of the turbulence that was to come at home. Her smart, low-cut dress, her brightly painted face, her city manners, the sinuous way she moved, and her free and easy laugh immediately established her as a scarlet woman. This sleepy village had seen nothing like it and talked about her in scandalized tones for weeks. Hans, the village simpleton, fell backwards, open-mouthed in astonishment, into the horse trough.

'I heard the news from the Baron and *had* to come to congratulate you,' Annemarie said, while Liese stiffened with moral indignation and hardly said a word while she was there.

She made up for it afterwards.

'So this is the business that keeps you in Frankfurt. She's your fancy woman, your painted whore. I might have known you wouldn't mend your ways . . .' and on and on.

It was no good my denying it. I was still attracted to women but I could *do* nothing with them; the Czech guards in the concentration camp had made sure of that. But Liese wouldn't believe me.

'You always were a liar,' she said. 'No faith, no morals, no standards at all – it's inevitable.'

She was right, but it distressed her far more than it did me. I did not tell her what my connection with Annemarie really was. She would have gone berserk if she'd known the truth.

The next day, as if to vindicate Liese's prophecies of doom, the German currency was reformed. At a stroke the money I had earned was reduced to one-tenth of its value. That was all that the old paper money was worth when converted into new Deutschmarks, but the old coins, which were so worthless that hardly anybody had them, could be exchanged on a one-to-one basis. The Baron, who had kept sacks of old coins from his slot machines, became a very rich man overnight. He became even richer when his factory burned down (he didn't know how it could possibly have happened, he said) and the insurance was paid in the new currency. There was no need of a partnership now; no papers had been signed and he did not plan to build another ceramics factory. He had other plans, he said, to make his money work for him.

I found it impossible to believe at first. I had trusted him and he betrayed our friendship.

'You mustn't take this personally, Martin,' he said. 'I like you. I've always liked you. But business is business. That's the way the cookie crumbles. You understand?'

'I understand all right, *Herr* Baron. I meant nothing more to you than a way to make a profit. I should have seen it, but I was blinded by friendship. All those presents for my family – the nylons, the chocolates, coffee . . . I thought you gave them as a friend. But you were just greasing the wheels of business. You've made a sucker out of me. You see?' I said, shouting at him, 'I've even begun to talk like you.'

'I'm thinking of opening a casino. I could find a place for you there.'

'Damn you and damn your casino! *Servus*, Herr Baron. If we ever meet again, I'll smash your face in.'

I stormed out and went home. I, who only yesterday had soared on dreams that touched the sky, had been brought crashing down to earth in flames. I felt exhausted, and angry, and dispirited. I felt *kaput* – finished. I wanted to get away from it all, from this hole of a village, this room with the view of the midden outside the window, Liese's scolding tongue, the skinflint farmers, and the whole damned tangle of living. But there was nowhere to go.

The next day I began writing this story.